ITHICA

Paul Sharpless

Sharpless Paper & Light

First published 2026

Published by Sharpless Paper & Light

ISBN (paperback): 978-1-7645003-0-2

ISBN (hardcover): 978-1-7645003-1-9

ISBN (ebook): 978-1-7645003-2-6

Cover design: Sharp Design Solutions / Paul Sharpless

Fiction notice

Author's Note

Ithica is a novel. It is a work of fiction.

I wrote this book in the shadow of things that, in my experience, are met with silence: the quiet power of institutions, the way reputations are manufactured, the way fear becomes policy, and the way people can be erased without the world noticing.

The events in this story are confronting and sometimes arrive without warning. That is intentional. In real life, the worst moments rarely announce themselves.

This story is told through a gay lens because my life is shaped by it.

My former partner of twelve years was Australia's first openly gay Royal Australian Naval officer. He became Deputy Director within an intelligence agency. In the world we moved through, that single truth can be used by people with power and access—people who don't need to be right to be dangerous.

The novel follows Anthea, an intelligence officer trapped inside a system of disappearances, corruption, and bureaucratic cruelty—a system that doesn't explain itself and punishes anyone who insists on reality. Anthea is not me. This is not a memoir. I chose fiction because facts can be buried, rewritten, or made to disappear.

The story carries dark, farcical humour for one reason: sometimes farce is the only language that keeps a mind intact. Comedy doesn't soften the horror. It makes it bearable enough to witness.

Names, places, timelines, and identifying details have been changed to protect the innocent, guilty and insane. Any resemblance to actual persons or events is coincidental.

In *Ithica*, nothing is safe. In an age of fake news, the truth is almost impossible to believe.

This book contains writing that some readers may find confronting, including depictions of violence, torture, murder and sex. Reader discretion is advised.

Dedicated to the memory of
Paul Ellis McKibbin

Acknowledgements

My deepest thanks to my husband, John Goldbaum, whose steady support, patience, and belief in this story carried me through every stage of writing. I could not have finished Ithica without you.

Chapter 1
Bandages

It was a noise Anthea hadn't heard for weeks.

No smell or fumes. No smoke. It reminded her of a person's neck cracking before death. That was work. Here, it was another tree branch snapping.

Her life had become routine. Part of that routine was falling asleep reading in the afternoon. Instinct and training meant she never moved her head when she woke. Only her eyes. She kept her head still while she slowly scanned the room, moving just her eyes.

All seemed well.

But well was pretty shit really. Her life was one of continual fear and loneliness. Flashbacks came hard and fast. Like now.

Her parents had both disappeared before she turned three. First her mother. Then her father. The state had taken her in, only for her to be neglected and molested in seventeen different care homes before her sixteenth birthday. After this, the care system discarded her to fend for herself.

Moving to Kings Cross, she soon learnt her local police station had been informed of her arrival. It seemed too coincidental when, one night walking home, a young handsome police constable stopped her after emerging from a dark laneway. She was too familiar with uniform insignia. Particularly cops and sailors.

He was eyeing her up and down, one hand on his belt, the other casually stroking his obviously hard cock.

"You should be careful around here, Anthea. There's a lot of crime, and I don't want to see a sexy girl like you participating ... taking part in?"

"Participating ..." she said, clumsily rolling her tongue around her mouth. "Officer. Sir. What part do you think I should be taking?"

Anthea dropped her gaze to the officer's erect cock and opened her mouth. That did it.

Holding her hand out, Anthea led the policeman into the laneway. She wanted to feel arms around her, be held, kiss the guy's lips and use her tongue. Like in the movies, and the videos her uncles had made of her. But she knew after this the police officer wouldn't hassle her, or he'd have her on speed dial.

In less than twelve months, Anthea saw a lot of Constable Andrew Tonelli. After their first child Georgio was born, Anthea said yes. They got married.

It was a difficult twelve months. In hindsight, it was the best twelve months of marriage she would ever have. Andrew was seldom home, "working late" or hanging out with his best friend Nathan. She knew what that meant but pretended not to.

At twenty-one, she was forced to join Ithica, a secret Australian intelligence agency. Andrew had "got her the job". The work was soul-destroying. Covering up and excusing an endless stream of bureaucratic and political abuse. She had tried to escape Ithica more than once. Last time, because her own colleagues had tried to kill her.

Now she was here.

An abandoned country shed outside Carcoar. Why Carcoar? Why anywhere? Because people left her alone. She told locals she'd escaped an abusive and violent marriage and just wanted peace.

She'd made the shed as weatherproof as she could. It looked abandoned and she liked that. The best part was the timber floor. It enabled her to dig under the floorboards.

Anthea looked around at the few furniture pieces she'd collected from roadside dumps and the local tip. She wasn't sure why she'd bothered. To feel like she was a person? Surely not. Like Carcoar, the furniture only had history, not comfort.

Anthea looked across at a local dog who had adopted her. Sitting on a cane chair opposite, for some inexplicable reason the kelpie visited her daily. Whatever the reason, Anthea found it difficult enough to provide food for herself.

She had escaped Ithica with only the cash in her purse. No aliases, no secret accounts, no income stream, no medical care. After being "promoted" at Ithica, she'd been officially warned her new boss was a psychopath, bipolar, and schizophrenic with anger management issues.

All this was obvious from day one. Her "promotion" also included a panic room adjacent to her desk.

When things go wrong, don't hesitate. Use it.

In hindsight, panic rooms are only useful if they're not rigged as remote-controlled death chambers. Hers was. She presumed previous personnel had discovered this the hard way.

She thought about the death chamber far too often. What she could have done differently. The precautions. She felt foolish and more depressed. How she, an intelligence analyst, had failed to notice what was happening right next to her.

Thinking about it made everything worse. Again.

The kelpie knew what came next.

"Time. It's time. It's time," Anthea said aloud.

She heard herself. Saying things three times had become a habit. Once, she'd told herself it was lucky. Now she'd looked at it more closely. It was stress. It happened just before things went catastrophically wrong.

The dog was already at the door.

"I'm not feeding you. No. No. No. Dead animals in a can. Catch your own. And don't bring them back here."

She bent down, scratched the dog's neck and spoke quietly.

"And don't bark. I'll see you tomorrow."

Slowly opening the shed door, as always, the kelpie was in no rush. He strolled out, ran a short distance, stopped, looked back at her, then took off up the hill toward the neighbouring farmhouse.

Their affectionate game. Same every day.

Anthea double-bolted the door. The action was symbolic and she knew it. She didn't like being alone. Worse, though, she remembered other analysts who had trusted people, then disappeared.

"Disappear. Disappear. Disappear."

She looked at her bed. A single mattress on milk crates. She never left the bed made. Appearances. It had to look like she'd left in a hurry. Even when the reality was far worse.

She opened a cupboard, then a badly concealed door in the bottom of the cupboard. She always feared someone else finding it.

She climbed down a rickety ladder into the narrow space she had dug out with her own hands. This was where Anthea spent most of her hours, day and night.

Anthea told herself she felt safe here.

"No. No. No." She corrected herself. "I don't feel safe here or anywhere."

She checked the tally scratched on the wall.

"This is day one thousand and fifty-seven since escaping."

The space was cramped but dry. She'd grown used to sleeping curled up.

Her "bed" down here was a single mattress of uncertain history. To the left of the mattress, a small television. Next to that, another screen showing various views inside and outside the shed. Finally, her computer.

She had anonymously linked the computer to Ithica's internal network. Defence and intelligence spent untraceable fortunes detecting threats from outside, and almost nothing tracking their own leaky, murderous insides.

Between disappearances, "suicides" and false identities, no one could calculate the true size of the workforce. Nor did anyone want to.

When Anthea disappeared from Ithica, she knew exactly what would have happened. Someone would be pocketing her salary.

Someone else her possessions. Someone would have claimed her superannuation. She'd seen it before.

Settling back against a cushion, she turned on the 6 pm news. Then she'd flip channels around the world for the next several hours, just like she used to do in the office.

The lead story was more Australian Defence spending on military hardware: planes, drones, submarines. Not personnel. It was the same old money grab. The figures were rubbery. No transparency. In a day or two, some intelligence chief would pop up to say they needed even more taxpayer money for unmentionable security threats.

She snorted when it was already the second story.

"That was quick," she muttered. "Government says no, so you send out your spruiking journos. Little embedders, doing your dirty work."

On screen, the head of ASIO pleaded for more money so Australians could feel safe.

Anthea looked around her bunker.

"Yeah. And how's that working? Fear, fear, all fear. That's all you've got."

She braced herself for the next segment. Politicians talking crap. She had to mentally armour up for that.

Instead, she flipped to the BBC. She was stunned.

Another person stabbed in London. One jab. Died instantly. Ordinary headline. Except she knew the man. Undercover for Ithica.

On her computer, she pulled up more detail. It had happened too fast. The footage showed an e-bike, a full-face helmet, one lunge. What bothered her was everything around it. The police, ambulance and coroner were practically loitering around the corner, waiting. The person's name was released instantly. No time to notify family or colleagues.

"There's no blue tent," she whispered.

No forensic tarp, no dignity. Just fast clean-up. It looked more like an operation than a crime scene. If Ithica was involved, the killer would never be found. That wasn't new. What was new was that they'd let the public see it all. His death was a message.

She just didn't know to whom.

She was about to switch to a camera feed outside when another story caught her. A plane crash. All 127 on board dead. An A320 to San Francisco had ploughed into a farmer's field.

She pulled up a passenger list. Airlines swore they didn't share them, but Australian intelligence had quietly learnt how to access their systems years ago.

Her system flagged two agents flying separately. Both were from the United Kingdom.

Then she checked the list of people travelling on false passports.

There it was.

A Vietnamese military general, his wife and their daughter travelling under fake identities. For years, he'd supplied Australian intelligence with information about Vietnam and its neighbours. When the risk grew too great, a deal had been made to relocate the family to Brisbane with new names and a fresh start.

At the last minute, Australian officials had stolen the resettlement funds and documents. The family had been left standing at the airport, exposed. Multiple countries wanted them dead.

Now 127 people were dead.

Anthea read the internal notes. Terrorists love a press conference. Intelligence agencies prefer silence.

She sat still, staring at the wall. She tried not to think, worried any thought or action would be the wrong one. It shouldn't be shocking her, but it was.

"No thinking. Nothing. Do nothing. Nothing."

Saying things three times wasn't working. She could feel it coming, that slow-rising pressure.

"Think nothing. Nothing. Nothing," she told herself, worried about another panic attack.

"Pep up. It's not that bad. You've got this. You can handle this. It's not like they want you dead."

She paused.

"No, that's wrong."

Another thought cut in.

"Hit yourself," Anthea said, tapping her cheek with her right hand.

"No. Harder. Don't be soft. You have to turn your mind off. Harder."

"Is there a reason for this?" she asked herself.

"Harder."

"Couldn't I tickle myself instead?"

"No. Don't do that. I'm having a panic attack. I'm feeling cold."

Her whole body ached now. Spine, neck, arms. She curled up under the blanket. She felt frozen, brittle, pointless.

"Hit your face harder. You're too soft."

She did as she was told.

"Again."

"Again."

"I hate you," she muttered.

"I am you," the voice replied.

She hit herself again, this time with a closed fist.

"Can we take a break? I need a break. I'm not listening to you."

"Hit yourself again."

"I'm not. I'm not doing it. I don't care who you are. I'm not listening. Every time. Every time you tell me to hit myself. It's never 'have a coffee' or 'open a can of food'. It's never anything pleasant with you. It's always 'hit myself'. I'm not listening."

Anthea realised she'd been yelling. She'd have to calm down. Immediately.

"If only I didn't watch the news," she whispered, knowing she'd just ruined another night's sleep.

She forced herself to breathe slower. Calm down. Get past the panic. It hadn't been that bad. She'd avoided the worst of it.

Then she saw it. A far bigger problem.

Behind the blanket hung at the far end of the dug-out, something moved.

Someone. But this was her secret space.

"It's mine. Mine. Mine," she said.

She'd planned for this, in theory. She knew they would come for her one day. She uncrossed her legs, then slowly reached with one hand for a lever on her left and a pistol on her right.

"You can come out now," she said, voice steady. "Slowly. Slowly. I've got the gun."

Nothing.

"I said come out. I'm not counting to three. I'll shoot you now."

"No," said a voice behind the blanket.

"No?" she questioned.

"No. It's Callam."

She stared as the man stepped around the blanket.

"No. You're not Callam."

"No. Yes. No. It's me, Anthea. Callam."

"And which part of you is Callam?" she asked. "Pull your jeans down around your legs."

"What?"

"You know. You heard. Now."

He hesitated, then unzipped his jeans and pulled them down.

He wasn't Callam. He wasn't gay. This man moved differently. Straight.

"You're wearing boxers," she said. Callam only wore boxers to parties; that was his total outfit, and they didn't last long.

"Sit," she said.

"Where?"

"On the sofa. In the jacuzzi. Where do you think? You want to be shot?"

"No. No. You can't shoot me."

"I can Superman. I can shoot who I like. Currently it's you."

"I have to take you back to Ithica," he blurted. "Not kill you."

"You're not making sense. You're not Callam. I have a gun. Think of it as a talking stick. They'll kill me if I go back. And then you."

"Anthea, I'm really Callam."

"You didn't get the memo. SET 24. Everyone died. Including you. You're dead."

"Same's true for you," he said.

"Touché."

"If I don't take you back, they'll kill me."

"If we go back together they'll kill us both. Choice is yours. Where do you want to be killed?" she asked.

"They've known you've been in Carcoar the whole time," he said.

"Don't get me involved in your death," Anthea snapped. "And they haven't."

Had they she wondered?

The idea that all her struggling, digging, hiding had been under surveillance the entire time? It might be a lie. It felt so cruel.

"Who says they want me dead? They're all a pack of liars!"

"Your old boss. Pete Jacobs. He's head now."

"What happened to Peter Jacobs?"

"Same guy. Calls himself Pete now. Says it sounds younger."

"The guy's a douche."

"Yeah, but if I don't take you back, he'll kill both of us."

"You keep saying that," she said.

Anthea had thought she'd prepared for this day. She hadn't.

She pointed out the lever to her left.

"You see that? Brings down a tonne of rock and soil. Fills the space. Kills us both."

"A bit overkill."

"I don't want to go back. Never."

"It's not our choice. You're the one who told me no one retires from Ithica. They kill you first. Have you got any water down here? I'm dry."

"What?" she asked.

"I'm thirsty."

"No tricks," she said, reaching for a water container. With the gun still in her hand, she fumbled and released a shot.

The sound was deafening in the confined space.

For a second she didn't know where the bullet had gone. Looking across, she saw blood.

He was clutching his chest. Anthea thought the worst. Her stomach dropped.

Then he grabbed his upper arm instead.

Panicking. Anthea pulled a long meat knife from under the bed. He tried to scramble backwards.

"Bandages," she said, cutting strips from the top sheet. "The bullet missed anything important."

"Fuckin' feels like it didn't," he groaned.

"It's a flesh wound. Size of a zit," she replied, wrapping the sheet around his arm, tight.

"There's whisky in my top pocket," he said, gritting his teeth. "Get it."

Anthea hesitated.

"I haven't got a gun. I have to take you back, not kill you."

She found a small hip flask where he said it was. Opened it, and poured whisky on the wound.

He yelled.

"I was going to drink it! What are you doing?"

"You're not Callam," she said.

"That's the least of our problems."

He was right. None of this was logical. If something made sense, it was probably the wrong thing to do.

He moved his right hand inside his jacket. Anthea, expecting another weapon, ripped his hand away and pulled out a second pistol. She pointed it at his chest.

"For God's sake," he said. "I brought you a present."

"A gun," she said flatly.

"No. No. You're the one with all the guns," he said, shaking his head. "I knew you wouldn't think it was me. It's not me. This is what they did. They changed my face. Made me thinner. No offence. At least they didn't give me a sex change like some of the others."

She hesitated and watched him throw a large hip flask in her direction.

"Whisky. Macallan Lalique. Seventy-two years old. We used to drink it together. Special occasions. Like when you got over your cancer."

"I didn't have cancer," said Anthea. "They claimed I did and removed my breasts."

"Yeah. That time."

If this was Callam, he'd know by now her "breast cancer" had been a lie. An excuse for unnecessary mutilation. They'd wanted her to suffer.

"I'm not playing this game," she said. "You can try all you like. I'm sure you read everything about Callam, and you know I don't know much about him. I'm not going back. So what's plan B?"

"They kill us both," he said softly.

"And you can live with that?"

"I'm scared," he blurted. "There. I've said it. And when did you last hear me being scared?"

She heard the trap in the question and remained silent.

"I don't think there's ... an alternative," he finished.

That wasn't the Callam she remembered. The real Callam would have said he had her back. That they'd got through worse. They'd screw Ithica before Ithica screwed them.

"You've got the whisky. Have some," he said. "It's open."

Anthea sniffed it and took a sip. It burned up her nose and down her throat. Some memories flooded back. Her with the real Callam. Watching torture videos. Being told to kill herself. Discovering her former husband was a drug lord.

That wasn't happening now.

Abruptly suspicious, she handed the flask back to him.

"There's no need," he said. "I've got this one."

"No, do it like we always do. One flask."

"I'm happy with mine."

"For old times, Callam. We share."

He took a sip. She couldn't be sure he swallowed.

"More," she said.

To her surprise, he drank again, then coughed at the strength of the whisky.

"We do have to go back Anthea," he said. "You know that. But we can make plans while we're driving. Take revenge. Steal what we need to get away properly."

The word revenge stuck out. There were too many. She'd have to prioritise, and then there was the question of how. The main ones had already banded together to protect each other. Except for Peter-now-Pete Jacobs, who only played for himself. Even if she took everything they had, it wouldn't be enough.

"You were trained in silent kill," he reminded her. "It's about time you used it."

She splattered the whisky she'd been savouring. It was true. Silent kill. Make the death look like something else. No traces.

Perhaps it was Callam. It made sense.

No.

She took another sip. Having had no alcohol for years, it went straight to her head. It felt ... good.

"Like so many others he's killed, Jacobs wants us dead too," the man said. "At least he's warned us."

"He's playing with us," said Anthea.

"He wants to fight you," the man said. "He wants to destroy you. You're a woman."

Chapter 2
Mettle

Emerging from her shed, Anthea saw Callam standing by the front of his car, an old silver Toyota sedan. She put a bucket of water down for the kelpie, hesitated, then got in. Callam remained outside, smiling despite his bandaged arm. She had no idea why. It was early, cold, and last night's whisky wasn't helping.

"Will it get us to Sydney?" she asked.

"Yes. And no. It doesn't have to."

She took that as no.

She was worried they were both going back to Ithica to be killed.

"They'll kill us?" asked Anthea.

"We've discussed this."

She wondered how she could be so trusting. She wondered the same thing many times. Somehow she always survived, even if it got worse each time. And the guy wasn't Callam. Or if he was, he looked and seemed too different.

It all felt futile. She understood why so many intelligence officers killed themselves.

Her recruiter's name was branded in her memory: Phillip Stackenwash. Hopefully an alias. Work for intelligence or we'll make your life hell, destroy you, and never leave you alone. Her husband had told her she'd better join. They needed the money.

Later, she'd found out people who refused recruitment simply disappeared.

She thought of killing herself so many times.

For a brief moment she'd been hopeful when yet another enquiry into suicides was announced. This one about Defence personnel. The Prime Minister, feigning concern, launched the inquiry. Then a hot mic caught him saying it was a "fuckin waste of Defence training money employing these idiots if they're going to kill themselves." That comment disappeared from the news cycle fast. Like most inquiries, it was a controlled circus. The media filmed broken people reliving their worst traumas, then cut to some politician or Royal Commission investigator saying the word sorry as if it were pain relief.

Anthea tried to think about something else. But no. At Ithica she'd kept an unofficial tally in her head. She still saw the young recruits being tortured, initiation rituals filmed from every angle, including the ones who died.

She recalled the lists of intelligence personnel secretly sent on overseas missions with no realistic way back. One or more a week disappearing. People on intelligence lists. All geniuses in their fields, forced to work alone on secret projects, then killed or vanished when they were no longer useful. They were fodder the day they were forcibly recruited.

She remembered one in particular, a young biological scientist. Davin. They'd talked, occasionally, in the corridors of Ithica. Then he was gone. When she tried to find him, she found instead his house, superannuation, and other assets now belonged to the man who was currently head of Ithica.

Pete Jacobs.

"You look worried," Callam said.

"No, everything's bliss, Callam. Couldn't be better. Why do you ask?"

She smiled, just a flicker. Overnight she'd decided to call him Callam, even if he wasn't. Let him think she'd fallen for it.

"McDonald's wrappers and bullet casings," she added, looking at the car floor. "You know I don't travel well. There are bullet casings. What the—"

"Put them on the back seat," he said. "You'll be more comfortable."

"It'd make more sense to get rid of them," she muttered, picking up the casings and twisting round to put them on the back floor. "There's a dead rat."

Callam turned the ignition. "We're off."

Anthea opened the glove box. "You got any travel-sickness tablets? Tranquillisers? Serious drugs? You must have painkillers. People will see I'm missing... especially in Carcoar."

"People at Ithica will talk to the local police. The cops will lie about your disappearance. Makes it easier for them," said Callam.

"Oh."

"Concentrate on revenge. It'll get you through," said Callam, pulling onto the back road, then the main road.

The sign said Sydne. The y was missing, shot out. Anthea told herself it wasn't an omen.

She sighed. The day she'd dreaded had arrived.

"I'm glad you decided to come back with me," said Callam.

She looked at him. Was he serious?

"So you get to stay alive a little longer," she said.

"Well yeah. And no. You haven't asked me about SET 24."

She hesitated. Was he for real? Was she meant to give him the long answer?

"You shouldn't tell me," she said. "For your own mental health. You don't need to tell me. You shouldn't try to relive it. You don't have to."

"But—"

"I know enough," she cut in. "Probably more than you do."

"I was there."

"Yeah. But it's like this. Say most people at SET 24 were murdered—"

"They were," Callam said.

"Well, forensically, gathering all the data from outside, we can see what really happened without talking to murdered people. Or you."

"That doesn't make sense."

Anthea was now more convinced he wasn't Callam. She tried again, a little slower.

"SET 24 was designed to fail. It was always going to. A lot of money siphoned off along the way. Obliterate, annihilate, whatever word you like. We don't need to speak to dead people—or you—to see what happened. We can interpret what happened. You can understand that."

"Well... maybe."

"So you don't have to know anything. Don't add to your PTSD. Or mine. The rest."

"When you put it like that," said Callam, nodding slowly, "they have to kill us."

"That's what I've been telling you," said Anthea, frustrated.

She saw she'd have to act on her own. She couldn't rely on this Callam. The previous one, yes. This version, no. She would have to get through alone.

She stared out at the eucalyptus trees, brown paddocks, the looping narrow roads. It looked like nothing was happening.

She watched everything: cars behind them, any drone overhead, helicopters, any pattern that felt wrong.

Looking at Callam, she guessed he was worried too. He'd been sent to fetch her. His life might end as soon as they got back.

He'd told her to think about revenge. She'd always tried not to. Thinking about it now, she started to list names. Apart from Pete Jacobs, who else? Who was protecting whom? Why send Callam? Why now?

Something big was about to happen. Whatever it was, Jacobs would need his favourite allies in the judiciary.

"You did well in your silent kill course," Callam said lightly.

Anthea tried not to smile. "We all did. We all said we were the best, better than anyone else. Except for the two who disappeared. And the one who supposedly killed herself. I think she was in-house practice.

We had a couple of young cops on the course. Thought it'd get them into intelligence. Stupid."

"By killing intelligence operatives?" asked Callam.

"Yes. The course lasted a week. Another week and most of us would have been dead. We were told not to mix. Trust no one. You couldn't. Our instructor said she was a dominatrix and a nurse. There were two other women and three guys on day release from prison. The three said they worked for intelligence." She shrugged. "You couldn't believe anyone."

"Did you talk to anyone?" he asked.

"No. Yes. Kinda. One of the prison guys. He came in civvies. Rugged, muscled, always flexing something—arms, legs, or several appendages simultaneously."

Callam stayed quiet.

"Don't think, just do it or they'll get you first, he said. Then he'd roll his tongue around his lips and go, 'Babe, is this what you really want?' while clasping his hands at the base of his balls and hard cock." She snorted. "Reminded me of my husband when I first met him."

"So he liked you?" asked Callam.

"He's straight. Living in an all-male prison."

"It's a start. What's his name?"

"Smothers."

"Smothers. You're making this up."

"I'm not. After each class the guards bussed them back."

"You need a guy..."

"We had sex," Anthea said.

"Where?"

"The same place you do. Washrooms. Bent over or sitting on vanities."

Remembering Smothers, Anthea felt like a cigarette. The killing classes were intense. The only breaks were for food or the bathroom. She'd met him on the way to the toilets. After that she told her tutor she had mild diarrhoea and needed frequent breaks. The tutor didn't care. She didn't care when class participants disappeared or "committed suicide" either. Sometimes she'd simply say, you did well.

Anthea's main problem in the killing classes was courage.

"You need mettle," the tutor told her. "Go and practice. Otherwise you're wasting your time and mine. With repetition your training will become spontaneous. Non-consequential."

"Can we stop at that gas station?" said Anthea, spotting a road sign and needing to get out of the car. The memories, the confined space, it was all closing in. "I need cigarettes."

"I didn't think it would take this long," she grumbled.

"We've only just left. We're taking back roads, crisscrossing the highway so no one sees us. And to avoid police."

Both now saw the old service station.

"I really do need cigarettes. And I know they'll kill me," she added.

He protested but gave in when she started talking again about how hard it was to go back to Ithica. Callam handed her three hundred dollars.

"Same problem for both of us," he said.

It was impossible to say how old or why the service station was built where it was. Newer bowsers were out front; the old ones rotted in a side yard with rusty trucks, dead cars, water tanks, and an old windmill that had collapsed in on itself.

Anthea went straight to the shop door and peered through the glass. It looked closed, but a young woman sat inside on an old grey velvet lounge, reading a book and smoking. When Anthea opened the door the smell hit her. The air was white with smoke. From outside you couldn't see it. Her first thought was fire detectors.

The woman didn't look up. She turned a page and kept reading.

"I'll be with you soon, honey," she said.

Anthea glanced at the wall behind the counter. The cigarette packs, usually hidden, were on full display. Callam would be annoyed at the delay. He hadn't wanted to stop.

Anthea deliberately dropped a pack of energy drinks she'd picked up.

The woman still didn't look up. Just turned another page.

"I love a good murder," she shrieked suddenly, springing to her feet.

Anthea saw now she was wearing lime-green sequin stilettos at nine in the morning. Her black leather shorts were unzipped.

"Tristerley Vijesk," the woman said, holding up the book. "The Open Carriage. I can't put her down."

"Three packets of Marlboro Reds," said Anthea.

"Tristerley. The open carriage. I just—"

"Three packets of Marlboro Reds," repeated Anthea. "No petrol."

"You're not from Daggers," the woman said, squinting at her.

"No," Anthea answered curtly.

"I thought you were our book club's new member. Our newest one lives over two hours away and still wants to come. We're reading The Open Carriage. Tristerley Vijesk. She used to do garden books and now she's murdering everyone."

"I wonder why," said Anthea. "Marlboros."

"Do you know Vijesk?"

"No. Marlboros."

The woman had no interest in selling cigarettes.

"We're closed today," she said. "I'm working from home. It's really my day off."

"But you're here."

"I live here. There's a closed sign out front."

"There is no closed sign."

"There is."

"No sign."

"There should be. It says, 'Have a great day, we're closed.'"

"No sign," Anthea said flatly.

"That's ridiculous. I must have forgotten to put it out. Sorry."

"I need three packets of Marlboros."

"We may have sold out. It's been very busy."

Anthea could see the Marlboro Reds clearly on the shelf.

"Perhaps you could look," she said. "I've got cash."

"I haven't opened the register," said the woman.

"I'll give you three hundred. I don't need change."

"I have to give you change."

"No one would know. Erase the cameras. Your choice."

"They don't work. Not connected."

Anthea hadn't felt this frustrated since Ithica. The entitlement. The casual lying. The meaningless "sorry."

"Should I just stand here and breathe your smoke? There's plenty of it."

The woman pursed her lipstick-heavy mouth. "I'm asking you to leave or I'll press the emergency button and bring the police," she said, moving toward the counter.

"And I'll take photos for my Instagram," said Anthea. "Show everyone how ridiculous you look."

She knew she had to stop the woman. It happened fast—instinctive, no marks, immediate faint. Count to twelve. No rush. Plenty of time. Heart attack.

She didn't touch the woman's skin directly. Part two: placement. Heart attack on the lounge. Struggle, try to stand in heels, fall onto the edge of the coffee table. Wipe prints. Finished. The training worked.

Then the Marlboros. Then Callam.

"Happy now?" Callam asked as Anthea put her seatbelt on.

Anthea said nothing.

She stared at the road and thought about what she'd done. It felt too easy. Her tutor had been right. Mettle. She worried the woman had lied about the cameras. If she lived there and it really was her lounge room, why have cameras? Why would anyone want surveillance where they slept?

Then she remembered how many people loved to be filmed.

Had there been any other cars at the station? Any customers? She couldn't remember. Callam had been stupid enough to park right at the bowser. If cameras worked, they would be in shot.

Anthea squeezed her fist until her nails cut her palm. Had she left marks on the woman? Was the woman truly dead? Maybe she'd come round. Too many unknowns.

"Just get over it," she told herself.

"Over what?" asked Callam.

"Nothing. Nothing at all."

She hoped he'd stay quiet. He did. She wanted to be far away from the servo, far away from everything. So when, half an hour later, he pulled into a churchyard, she flinched.

"Why are we stopping?" she snapped. "We don't need to. What's wrong?"

"We're changing cars."

"Here? At a church. With a graveyard."

The stone building was abandoned. Headstones leaned to one side; a line of pine trees behind them made a windbreak. Through the trunks she saw two cars. A setup.

"Go and chill," said Callam. "Check out the gravestones. I'll swap cars."

She almost argued, then stopped. Maybe it wasn't a setup. Maybe it was just anxiety. Killer's remorse.

Wandering between the stones, she didn't expect to see her own surname.

TONELLI. Edith Tonelli, 1880–1903.

She had no idea who the woman was. Her husband had never mentioned relatives. No parents, no siblings, no photos. Nothing.

Anthea realised she was edgy. No that was her.

It was natural she jumped when turning to see a man immediately behind her in the graveyard. No she was too jumpy. She hadn't heard him approach. No Excuse. He was staring at the stone in front of him: JOYCE SMATLIEFER.

Anthea knew the surname. She knew him.

"There's normally nobody here," he said, still staring down. "No one comes here."

"I hear the church and graveyard is being sold," Anthea lied, watching him.

"To be expected," he sniffed. "Paying for priests and boys."

"Nothing's certain," she said.

"Religion," he snorted. "We parked Mother here. Across the road from their property."

"It's lovely land," said Anthea.

"It's shit. I renamed the property Cacare. Latin for shit."

She stayed silent. She was sure now. Nigel Smatliefer. The corrupt barrister made judge to avoid prosecution. The homophobic family court judge who didn't believe in relationships but still decided other people's. The man who falsified documents and lied in court, then used his robe to destroy even more lives. No one stopped him. Least of all other judges.

Ordinarily, his decisions would be appealed. But law was so expensive, most victims never got that far.

Anthea watched Nigel clutch at his head. Her next thought: a brain aneurysm. It was quietly executed. He fell forward towards her. She moved. He came to rest on his mother's gravestone.

If only she'd done it sooner, she thought, for all those ruined lives—just because he could.

Her tutor was right. Mettle.

She walked back around the church. Callam was bent over the engine of an old white Mazda.

"Everything's good?" asked Anthea.

"Yeah. It'll get us there." He wiped his hands. "No Wi-Fi, no cameras, no tracking devices. Get in."

She felt oddly relieved. The ancient car comforted her. So did the fact he hadn't asked what she'd been doing. Maybe he hadn't seen her with Smatliefer. Someone bad was dead.

They drove on. The fields were green, cattle standing motionless, dams full. Farmhouses with neat gardens sat under rows of trees. Newer houses, bigger and bigger, dotted the hills. The state forest they entered looked healthy. All this during a severe drought.

It didn't make sense.

Anthea watched the dashboard clock. Time moved slower out here. It was faster in Carcoar.

At ten am she turned on the radio. A local country station. The lead story was closure of a cattle yard. Then: breaking news. A family court judge found dead. More details to come.

"That's fast," Anthea said before she could stop herself.

Callam stayed quiet. When she asked how long till they got there, he didn't answer. He kept weaving across the highway, back roads, detours. Stretching the trip.

She wasn't alone in Carcoar anymore. She was heading back into crowds.

Why had she gone to Carcoar? She wished now she had hid out much closer. No further than a suburban train journey. Forty-five minutes max. Nothing with country.

Agitated more, she could feel an attack coming. She wouldn't reach Ithica.

She checked the rear window. The back roads were narrow. Two cars appeared, side by side, racing towards them with their lights flashing.

At first she couldn't make out the models. As they got closer she saw one was a marked police car, the other an unmarked Special Branch sedan, both lights going, both doing ridiculous speed.

"Get off the road. Hide," she yelled at Callam.

Seeing the lights in the rear-view mirror, Callam swung into a firebreak. There was no time to waste. The two cars screamed past, side by side, like it was a drag race. She counted at least three people in each.

They watched them disappear over a rise.

"Something's happening," said Callam. "Why did you say hide?"

She didn't answer. She couldn't be sure Smatliefer was dead so soon on the news. The theatre woman. Country cops racing around. It had to be coincidence. She told herself she was overreacting.

Callam turned the car around and resumed driving. She was still telling herself it was all coincidence when they rounded a bend and saw three cars blocking the road.

Her first thought: we're caught.

Then she counted. At least seven police cars. Four unmarked vehicles. Numerous motorbikes. All lights flashing. Too many people to count. Six officers stood behind trees drinking beer. Behind them, two cops were having sex on a motorbike. Four more smoked joints. An undercover officer racked a line of coke on a bonnet; a female cop waited to snort hers. No, she was providing it.

Two small children, naked—a boy about three, a girl seven or eight—were being photographed.

Anthea felt her stomach lurch. Her ex-husband was a cop. He'd used their children the same way. Then sent her the video.

"What the fuck," said Callam, braking hard.

A rotund officer stood in front of his car, hands on hips.

Anthea and Callam stared. The smell of marijuana floated through the open windows. The sniffer dogs nearby were going crazy at the smell.

"We got you," the rotund cop shouted. "Stay in your car. Don't get out or I'll shoot you both."

"I don't want to be shot again so soon," murmured Callam. "Do what he says."

"There're no number plates," Anthea whispered. "No car numbers. No name badges."

"They normally hunt in packs," said Callam. "He's not using his radio."

"Are they cops?" she asked.

The officer stared at them for a long time, then slowly waddled over to Callam's window, unwrapping a chocolate bar from his pocket.

"What's happening, Officer?" Callam asked.

"You tell me. Terrible hurry to get somewhere. Terrible hurry. Licence."

Callam handed it over.

"And your wallet and phone."

Reluctant, Callam gave him the wallet and mobile—both part of his false identity. The cop stepped back and flicked through.

"Seven hundred dollars. Thanks," he said. "Business cards. Your photo. An accountant. You take people's money."

Anthea was baffled. Three motorcycle cops strolled up. One smashed the headlight. Another cracked the rear window. The third took out his pistol and fired into the back door. It had a silencer; there was barely a sound.

"What's wrong, Officer?" Anthea asked, politely.

"Shut up. You're next," he said. "Didn't see you at first. Were you down giving him a blowjob?"

She flinched but didn't react. She knew how corrupt the state police were. Drugs, extortion, the odd murder, prostitution, children.

"Your bag and mobile," he ordered.

She handed him her bag. He dumped it on the bonnet.

"Where's your phone?"

"I don't need one," she said. "I don't have one."

He sifted through her things, then picked up her identity card.

"What's this? Where's your driver's licence?"

"I don't have one. That's my ID."

He stared at it, then passed it to another officer. That man wandered off into the trees and interrupted a woman having sex with two men. A young naked, good-looking cop came back a minute later and spoke quietly to the rotund one.

"They're getting a warning," he said.

Callam stayed silent.

The rotund cop started writing a ticket, but another man—a naked officer with an erection—strode up and grabbed the pen.

"Just get rid of them," he said looking at Anthea and Callam. Then jogging back into the trees to resume having sex.

Anthea watched his buns as he ran.

Moments later he was running back again, still naked, still hard.

"I mean have them disappear," he said. "Like, let them go."

"Which?" the rotund cop asked, opening another chocolate bar.

"Let. Them. Go."

The rotund cop belched.

"I'm trying to get a promotion," the naked cop said, absently rubbing himself.

"I'm sure my sister will give it to you," the rotund one replied.

The younger man stiffened. "No names. No."

"Sorry Rod," the cop said quickly. "Nobody heard that."

"You'll be digging your own grave one day," the naked man said, then ran back into the forest.

Anthea looked around. Pointless memorising faces; the force would close ranks. Whatever this was—drug operation, abuse ring—it wasn't stopping here.

"You heard him," the rotund cop said. "We're letting you go. But we know where you live. I'd be careful if I was you." He tossed the car keys at Callam.

Callam turned the car around and drove back the way they'd come. Once they were clear of the flashing lights he stopped, got out, and swapped the number plates. Then he opened Anthea's door, peeled back a panel beside her seat and revealed a hidden compartment: wallet, mobile with a different identity, and a pistol with silencer. He dropped them into the console and kept driving.

They said nothing. Anthea turned on the radio.

A few minutes later another police car roared past in the opposite direction, lights flashing, heading to the party they'd just left.

"Why the lights?" Anthea asked. "There really are too many police in this state. You can't go anywhere without tripping over a bunch of them."

"Like mosquitoes," said Callam.

"Yeah. Why were they giving you a warning?" asked Anthea.

"You know why." he said.

Anthea said nothing.

"Your husband's high up the greasy pole now."

"I don't know."

"Yes you do."

She didn't want to talk about her ex.

The radio cut to breaking news. Justice Barry Paramount found dead in his swimming pool.

"Two judges?" said Callam.

"Yes, that's right. Paramount and Smatliefer both dead this morning," said the female announcer. "It's a bad day for justice."

"I'm not sure about that, Melody," a male radio announcer replied. "Maybe some of your listeners could ring in."

"I'm not sure about that, George," she responded. "You know we're not allowed to talk about judges on this station."

"Why's that, Melody?"

The station went dead.

They waited. Nothing.

Callam switched to another local station.

"An owner of a gas station at Weeping Falls was found dead this morning," said the news announcer. "She is thought to have had a heart attack."

"We went there this morning," said Callam.

"Where?"

"Weeping Falls. You wanted to stop for—"

"It wasn't there," Anthea said quickly.

"Yes. I remember the name."

"No. No-no. No-no. No-no."

"No-no. Was she smoking?" he asked.

"I don't think so. She may have lit one."

"You smelt like cigarettes when you got back in the car."

"Vijesk," said Anthea. "She was reading The Open Carriage."

"Did you kill her?" asked Callam.

Anthea hesitated.

"Yes. It was quick. No pain. Looked like a heart attack. They said that on the news."

"Are you giving the station credit for picking heart attack?"

"Not at all."

"And Smatliefer?" he asked.

"What about Smatliefer? He's dead."

"Well, he is now. I saw you two talking."

Anthea turned her head away and stared out the window. She needed time.

"Isn't it enough I'm going back to Ithica with you so you won't be killed?" she said quietly. "I'm trying to keep us alive. I'm doing this for us."

"You can't go around murdering people... for me."

"What murders? Heart attack and a brain aneurysm," she said firmly. "Perception versus reality 101 at intelligence. You'd do well to remember that."

"You're telling me," said Callam. "I'm surprised they didn't kill you years ago Anthea."

She knew better than to answer.

"Three hours in a car with you," he muttered. "I need time. We're going to Gier's."

"What, or who, is Giers?" she asked.

Chapter 3
Watch for Snakes!!!

Callam watched Anthea twitching, fidgeting, trying to sit still while her mind spiralled. He hadn't expected driving her back to Ithica to be this exhausting. She was never going to trust him. After knowing she'd killed at least two people already that day. He was starting to think he'd be next.

It was fortunate Gier had bought a small farm nearby. Callam hadn't seen Gier in over a year, but now he felt the pull — he needed someone sane, someone grounded. He had never recovered from surviving SET 24. After the murders, after escaping, nothing had made sense. He needed to see Gier. Level-headed Gier, who might tell him what to do before Ithica finished them both.

Perhaps Anthea was right. Maybe they should disappear. Go somewhere, but with what? Neither of them had stashed away provisions. If they ran, Ithica would hunt them down. He was thirty-five; she was forty-eight. Their lives were over the day they'd joined Ithica.

Callam remembered his first day. His supervisor lecturing him like a preacher:

Justice. Fairness. Everybody gets a fair go in Australia.

The man was serious. And this was said to Callam after he'd been forcibly recruited. Join or die.

It got worse. The following week he and three other recruits were mid-morning sent "camping". They were put in cages and dumped separately in dense bushland somewhere outside Sydney. That night several men dragged him out of the cage and engaged in what they said was intelligence recruit initiation training. Torture.

A dirty ball gag was forced into his mouth, tasting of previous victims. His captors seemed to have a fascination with his arse, genitals and nipples.A blow to his head resulted in pain so sharp his vision blurred.

Two of the cages were empty on their return trip to Sydney. Blood dripped through the cages onto the truck floor.

"Tell anyone and you'll be back camping," threatened one of the hooded guards. Callam avoided sex for weeks after the torture. Too afraid his internal bleeding would resume.

Maybe travelling with Anthea wasn't so bad after all.

Anthea squinted ahead. Callam had told her to look for the property sign.

"S T U D S," she exclaimed as they approached the gate.

Callam grinned. He knew the sign well — Gier had welded the letters into his bedhead years ago, holes in the wrought iron perfect for handcuffs and ropes.

Callam felt a strange sense of coming home. He hoped Gier would feel the same.

He remembered Gier was a dancer at Pythons Gay Pole Club when he disappeared. All the dancers were terrified they'd be next. Police didn't care. He's gay, homos always go missing, we hear he's a big guy, he can look after himself.

Then whispers Gier was in a high-security jail. FOI refused all inquiries — even saying releasing information could "jeopardise the government in any future court cases." People assumed his Supreme Court judge father had arranged for Gier to be "put away" on trumped-up charges.

Now, driving up the long tree-lined driveway, Callam saw Gier standing on the house steps — and he looked even better than before. More handsome. Gier's face lit up.

"Cal... Cal... I wondered who... we don't get many visitors," said Gier, pulling him into a hug. "I missed you, man."

Callam kissed him. Hugged him longer than appropriate. Smelled him again. Same scent, same warmth.

"You've been working out."

"It's a farm. We work out in a lot of ways... you want to see?"

"Totally."

"You've got a passenger?"

"Who... Oh yeah... Anthea," said Callam. "I forgot."

"I'll stay here," Anthea muttered.

"There's food in the house," Gier said vaguely, his eyes fixed on Callam. "Come on. You've gotta see this."

He dragged Callam toward the back of the property like an excited teenager.

"Where we going?" Callam laughed. This was the old Gier — chaotic, charming, distracting him from death for five minutes. Callam hesitated, then admitted, "We could have been great together."

Gier smiled. "I know."

Walking along the creek, Callam was smitten again by Gier pulling him along, Gier's hand holding tight.

Tall grass brushed their legs.

"Watch for snakes," warned Gier, squeezing Callam's hand tighter.

Callam ignored him. Then froze.

"It looks like a children's jumping castle... in timber."

"It is... sort of," said Gier, kissing him hard, pulling off his T-shirt, getting on his knees to tug down Callam's shorts.

"Your turn," said Callam.

Moments later they were naked, Gier slinging Callam over his shoulder like a trophy.

"To the castle!" said Gier.

Hung over Gier's shoulder, Callam looked down at Gier's abs and erect cock. He loved this guy. All the sex they'd had before. Callam was then pushed against the castle door before being dropped onto a large mattress full of cushions.

Callam stared up at the castle's timber ceiling, turret and windows. Gier bombarded him with cushions before lying next to him.

"The bandage?" Gier queried.

"It's nothing."

Callam felt his body somehow being hoisted to a side wall. He'd been tied up without realising it. Chains made the sound of a drawbridge being drawn. Callam was going along for the ride, feeling secure he was with Gier.

It wasn't such a hot day, but before long both men were sweating over each other, climaxing only to climax again and again. Neither wanting to stop, only continue.

Callam somehow fell back on the mattress and Gier collapsed next to him. Both waited to hear the other speak.

"I never imagined you to be a stud farmer," said Callam.

"I never thought so either... I'd rather have one pole than a whole fence of them."

Callam laughed. "That isn't true... we... I... was worried when you disappeared... no one could find you. I missed you more than ever."

"That was my father's doing... he wants us gone. Like my mother."

"I know she got nothing."

"It got worse. She discovered he had a Thai girlfriend and three kids in Bangkok. My brother told him he'd go public. My father promised to put him away for life. Jail or asylum. He killed himself. Wasn't really him by then."

"So... you escaped."

"Trying to. My father's an arsehole... everyone knows that. And if you don't, you soon find out when you're before him in court."

Gier leaned over Callam's face. Sweat dripped into Callam's eyes. At first he thought they were Gier's tears. Understandable.

"You're staying the night?"

"Yeah... I need a rest," Callam responded.

"No fuckin way. You have to meet my saviours. They'll be home now."

Both men kissed again.

"I haven't asked how you're going," said Gier.

"What is this... pillow talk?" said Callam.

Callam hesitated.

"About the same as you. Worse if Anthea has killed your two friends," said Callam, unconsciously touching his bandaged wound.

"You said it was a scratch."

"Yeah. From a bullet."

Gier laughed, then realised. "You're serious."

"Yeah... she's practising for when she returns to work."

Gier was noticeably stressed. Jumping up from the mattress, he fumbled into his shorts, lost his balance, fell back on Callam, then scrambled off.

"Let's go... you should have told me... you should have." Gier ran out the door. Callam watched him slip on the wet grass, recover, then run toward the house. Sunset. The afternoon gone.

Rushing back, Callam wondered if Anthea had killed Gier's saviour friends. It was possible. Three years of isolation had made her more problematic, angrier.

Returning to the house, all the lights were on but no one was there. Running through the rooms, Callam thought the worst. He yelled out Gier's name.

Silence.

Gier would never forgive him — if he were still alive. Running out a bedroom side door, Callam saw lights in two sheds.

He yelled again.

Still silence.

Surely Anthea hadn't killed all three.

Running through one shed — nothing. In the next he could see his car on the far side, and Anthea sitting on the back seat, door open, smoking a cigarette.

"What have you done?" yelled Callam.

Anthea smiled. "I had a drink with the boys."

Thinking the worst, Callam was horrified.

He hesitated. Would he have to kill Anthea? Would she kill him first? He couldn't be sure they were all dead. And how? So soon? He hesitated — hoping somehow he'd hear a voice.

And he did. A man he didn't know, similar build to Gier.

"Tim," the man said.

"Wow," Callam said, staring at the rugged man. "Looks like you lift cows."

"Anthea insists on sleeping in the car," said Tim, ignoring the compliment. "Jason and Gier are still getting blankets from the caravan."

"Terrific... great news... couldn't be happier," replied Callam. He was exuberant seeing two men return with bedding, though Gier gritted his teeth at Callam. Gier was still angry.

"This is Jason, Cal. You've met Tim," said Gier.

"Anthea insists on sleeping in the car," said Jason, handing over bedding. Wearing shorts, Callam noticed Jason had a prosthetic right leg.

"I insist, guys... I'll be more comfortable... you'll be more comfortable," said Anthea.

"Definitely," exclaimed Gier. "We... all... have to be comfortable."

"Okay... then that's settled. Anthea will stay in the car... sleep," added Callam.

"I promise," whispered Anthea, seeing Callam's frown.

Leaving her in the car, the four men returned to the house. Callam looked back — Anthea rearranging her bedding. Suddenly he remembered the pistol still in car.

Too exhausting. It could wait.

Back inside, Callam looked again at Tim and Jason.

Tim tossed him a beer. "So Gier showed you the castle?"

"Yeah."

"Did you see the drawbridge?"

"I felt it," Callam replied.

All four men grinned.

"Then welcome," said Tim.

"Did Gier show you the barn?" asked Jason.

"Which barn?" questioned Callam.

"You didn't see it?" Jason said smiling.

"We ran out of time," said Gier. "I haven't seen Cal since Pythons."

"You worked there too?"

"No," Callam said quickly, not knowing what to say next.

"He works for Ithica," Gier said hesitantly.

"Oh no... that's terrible," replied Jason. "I lost my leg in the navy, but Ithica would have killed me and covered it up."

"True," said Callam, then hesitantly asked, "Can I ask how?"

"Yes... My Commander shot me in the leg," said Jason. "He was drunk. They sent me to the military hospital. I got worse, a lot worse. I think they tried to kill me."

"They did, Jason," said Tim. "And Graves became a Captain, then quickly a Commodore when worse stories of his abuse surfaced."

"Graves?" repeated Callam.

"Jason hasn't received anything from the military or Veterans Affairs except threats," said Tim. "Unlikely he ever will."

"Tim and I saw what was happening to Gier," added Jason. "We had to help him. We're a throuple."

Callam remained quiet looking at Gier.

"We bought the farm together," said Tim. "It's a lot easier with three of us... throuples are the future of farming."

Callam laughed — until he realised they were serious.

Walking to the fridge for more beer, Tim said, "We're thinking of doing farm stays."

"We are not," Jason said firmly.

Not feeling so comfortable for such a long time, Callam wiped a tear from his eye. He hoped no one saw.

Tim did, though — and smiled.

Despite everything, these three men were helping each other.

Callam could see they genuinely loved each other. All three. They moved around the room, sitting close to one then another.

As the night went on, so did their conversations. Hours passed. Gier and Tim settled on one sofa and Callam and Jason on another.

The four of them rested, arms and legs entwined. Jason had fallen asleep in Callam's arms. Callam didn't dare move.

"You want to know, don't you," whispered Gier. He didn't want to wake Jason.

"Know what?" asked Callam. Tim looked asleep — or pretending.

"You know... you should stay."

"I can't stay... I've got that mad woman in the car."

They smiled at each other.

"I can drive her to Sydney," offered Gier.

"I have to take her. Orders."

"Then come back after."

"I wish," admitted Callam.

The room was warm, safe, full of low breathing. He drifted asleep entwined with bodies. It was bliss.

Waking. Callam wondered where he was at first. Rousing to the sound of three cocks. Funny. The farm had three roosters.

Jason was already up and the smell of coffee filled the air. Callam thought Jason was in the kitchen, but hearing the toilet flush, saw him emerge from the bathroom.

"They'll be asleep until eight," said Jason.

"But you're farmers."

"And that's why we don't have milking cows," replied Jason.

Both laughed.

"We should be getting away," said Callam.

"I'd be running away," replied Jason.

"No. Back to Sydney. Ithica doesn't do AWOL."

Hearing the dominant cockerel again, Jason asked if the three cocks kept him awake.

"Not at all." Jason explained the third had been introduced after he came to the farm. "That way we all have one. Though mine caused a lot of drama.

Jason handed him a second cup. "For Anthea."

Walking together to the car, there were no signs of activity. The car windows were open. Anthea was still asleep.

Then Callam saw it — blood.

They both stared at Anthea: blood dripping down the front of her T-shirt. Her eyes closed. Callam shook her arm.

She was alive.

"Again," he said. "Who's?"

"What?" she mumbled.

"You can't stop. Can't help yourself," said Callam.

Anthea squinted. "Good morning to you too. Yes, I slept well. Thought you'd sleep in. In Gier."

"You've got blood."

Anthea looked down — horrified.

"It's not mine."

"It would be easier if it was," said Callam. "Can you feel wounds? Organs missing?"

"There's more on the opposite seat," said Jason. "Oh — a blood trail to the boot."

"I've been here all night," protested Anthea. "Only left to pee in the bushes."

"Stay. Don't move," said Callam.

Callam and Jason went to the back.

Callam opened the boot.

A body. Naked. Torn apart. Unrecognisable. It reminded Callam of a shark attack he'd seen. Perhaps it was an animal. No.

"Anything there?" called Anthea.

"Nothing you need to see."

"That's good."

Callam whispered, "This isn't Anthea. She couldn't do this. Not strong enough."

"Who then?" asked Jason.

"Let's see what she says."

Back at the car door, Callam laid his shirt over the blooded seat and sat.

"There's a body in the boot," said Jason.

"You said there's nothing there."

"Nothing left," replied Jason.

"It's not my body," said Anthea. "Somebody else did this... Who knows we're here?"

"Hang on," said Jason.

"So much for your back roads," said Anthea.

"If you hadn't been silently killing people, we'd be at Ithica by now."

"You know I hate travelling," Anthea replied quickly.

"What's that got to do with killing people?"

"You're blaming me for the boot?"

"No. I'm asking you to stop killing people."

"You're blaming me."

"I'm not blaming you for the boot. You're throwing a tantrum. I should drop you at a kindergarten."

"See? You are blaming me."

"Kids," Jason snapped. "Stop. They could be watching."

All were silent.

"Should we go to the police?" asked Jason.

"No," said both instantly.

"Only if you want to buy drugs," added Callam. "Ithica's behind this. It's a warning."

Jason shook his head. "Take a vehicle if it helps. I don't get why they torment people. Don't they have actual work?"

"We spend most of our time worrying how they'll kill us," said Anthea. "And who they've already killed."

Jason nodded slowly.

"Nauseous, afraid, waiting for them to finish you — that's normal," added Anthea.

"We need to go," said Callam.

Anthea peeled off her shirt. "Burn or bury this," she said looking at Jason.

Jason immediately offered his.

She took it.

"I'm sorry, Jason," said Callam. "I shouldn't have come."

"You shouldn't have come where?" said Gier, appearing.

"Here. I shouldn't have brought Anthea."

"I'm glad you came," Gier said softly.

"There's a dead body in the boot," said Callam. "Unrecognisable."

"Change cars?" suggested Gier.

"I already asked," said Jason.

"No," said Callam. "If police stop us, they'll be told to say nothing. Ithica's problem."

"It's Ithica overkill," said Anthea.

Chapter 4
Little Treasure

Back on the highway, Anthea was forever noticing police vehicles. Some parked on the roadside checking speeds. Others selling speed. She'd seen it in files at Ithica. More police and undercover cars were partially hidden behind bushes or buildings. It was menacing to Anthea, especially with the dead, mutilated body in the boot.

Callam was quiet. They'd argued earlier. He'd told her she'd jeopardised his life by randomly killing people.

"Are you—" asked Anthea.

"No. I'm still not talking to you," said Callam.

"It seems you are?"

"I said fuckin' no. We're going directly to Ithica so you can't kill anyone else."

"It's practice," said Anthea, knowing she might have over-practiced.

She was finding it difficult—impossible. What was the correct thing to do? Was any answer correct? She'd gone from thinking about suicide to thinking about survival. Both seemed equal. No middle ground. Callam collected her. It felt like a roundup of cattle for the slaughterhouse.

"What, and you did it to help us?" said Callam.

Anthea ignored him. They were both beyond help. She and Callam would disappear like all the others at Ithica. She was forever remembering people who had vanished. More people every week. It was impossible to understand how so many did nothing, remained silent, didn't want to know. They stayed quiet, like the police.

"When we reach Ithica we might be locked up or killed immediately. Both of us. You'd do well to be ready. You're not the prodigal son," she said.

"I know that Anthea. But we're not at Ithica. I'm trying to make no mistakes driving and not draw attention to ourselves. Dead body... you remember."

"Your driving isn't going to make any difference. Ithica knows where we are. They put the corpse in the boot," said Anthea.

Callam stayed quiet, thinking about what she'd just said.

"Ithica made it clear with the corpse," he said. "Could've been a dead sheep. They didn't have to kill someone specially."

"Do you think police will stop us?" asked Anthea.

"I have no idea. You're really rattled... how would I know? My bet is no. I think the police have made us code 10–25. Do not have contact with this vehicle or occupants."

"I know what code 10–25 is, but the police stopped us yesterday," said Anthea.

She wasn't surprised by the police the previous day. There were often reports and photographs at Ithica of New South Wales police—sometimes even in police cars—doing their side hustle of selling drugs to locals. In some country areas, drugs were a huge problem.

"Their radios were off yesterday, remember... get it together, Anthea. We'll be at Ithica soon," said Callam.

"Then what... haven't you told me? Why are we still alive?"

"Look... I'm forced to take you back... if you'd bothered to do your job correctly you would have stashed away a nest egg. We wouldn't be having this conversation. So for God's sake, get it right this time."

"I'll do it," she said.

"Squirrel away everything you can. You're a fool if you don't."

"I know, I know..."

"Well bloody do it," Callam said angrily.

Anthea remained silent. She'd been stupid. She'd been too busy watching other people disappear or be killed.

"Hang on... I forgot. I did put a stash away... but Jacobs took it."

"It couldn't have been Jacobs. Normally he takes it and kills the person."

"You're right... but... it was Jacobs," she said.

"Get resourceful, Anthea... you could've been anywhere in the world besides Carcoar."

She remained quiet. Callam was correct. She'd been stupid.

Approaching the city, parts of the highway were familiar. Entering the new road tunnels, all that changed. The long, bored-out tunnels went for miles. Anthea somehow felt more comfortable now. It reminded her of walking around Ithica with its labyrinth of passageways, most with concealed entrances and secret rooms behind. This was the world she felt comfortable in—not seeing other people or what was happening to them. She told herself she was preoccupied with her own work. These were lies. She'd been afraid to put her head up, like most people at Ithica.

When Callam finally emerged from the tunnel, Anthea saw many new parts of the city ahead of her. She left it to Callam to drive wherever they needed to go but was surprised when he announced "we're here."

It had changed. Ithica used to be part of the Navy base. Now it was located in high-rise residential and office towers. Anthea could see the casino at the end of the road.

"What happened?"

"To what?" asked Callam.

"Why have we stopped? I thought we were going to Ithica," said Anthea, worried the whole journey was a trick.

"Ithica. Your fire destroyed it."

"It wasn't my fire. Jacobs tried to drown and gas me in my panic room."

"Word is you tried to burn the place down."

"It didn't make the news..."

"Ha. Of course it didn't. And moving didn't either."

"Right... so which is the lucky high-rise? Who are the lucky residents waiting to be bombed?"

"That one," Callam said, pointing to the residential building in front. "Levels six to twelve of forty storeys, with our own entrance," he said, pointing to a roller door at the far right and what looked like a fire exit next to it.

"Oh, that's clever... the two street security cameras out front... so the whole world knows who goes in and out. I suppose they're Chinese cameras."

Callam remained quiet.

"Ithica was underground for a reason—many reasons. It's a bat cave, not a children's birthday party... sticking it in a residential building... windows, X-rays, and the rest... no protection," said Anthea.

"I know, I know, Anthea."

"So all the residents in the building are monitored, which wouldn't be necessary if Ithica was underground."

"I know," repeated Callam. "Get off your milk crate... are you ready? Because once we go in here there are no second chances... we survive or we don't."

Anthea screwed up her face. Callam took that as yes and drove to the large unmarked roller door. He pressed his thumb on a side panel and the door opened.

Moving into the garage, Anthea saw the dark tunnel corkscrewing down several levels before flattening into separate car spaces divided by concrete walls. Despite the building being new, several lights were out and there was a smell of damp or something else she couldn't identify.

Matter-of-factly, Callam pointed at the lift doors and told Anthea to go first.

"Stand in the lift and security will do the rest. You'll be going up to authorisation first... see you after that."

Anthea didn't question Callam. Looking back, he was already gone.

Approaching the lift, she saw its doors open. Stepping inside, there was no panel, and the doors closed immediately.

Suddenly the lift lights became extremely intense—piercing like X-rays—and the lift moved. Down, not up, as Callam had said.

When the lift finally stopped its descent, it seemed to travel to the right. Then the back of the lift opened—doors she hadn't known existed.

The space in front of her seemed cavernous and grey. No walls or ceiling—just a floor. She stepped out.

"Sit," said an Asian female voice.

"Sit—I said sit—sit sit," the voice repeated sharply.

Before Anthea even realised, she was lying on the floor.

"You have pippers."

"What?"

"Pippers," the woman repeated.

Anthea said no—she didn't understand the term.

"Good. That is correct. You are not to have pippers on you at any time."

It seemed Callam had lied. She was going to be tortured. Anthea thought of past times—especially the last.

Ahead, the Asian woman now sat at a desk with an empty chair.

"Sit."

Anthea moved quickly to the chair. The woman studied her computer screen.

"You are claiming to be an Anthea Tonelli."

"I am Anthea—"

The woman interrupted sharply. "You are claiming to be an Anthea Tonelli." The woman interrupted sharply.

Anthea felt annoyed. "I am not a... thing."

"Digital. You are a thing. You are part of everything... or nothing. No digital footprint, no digital recognition—no recognition."

Anthea understood. She'd read about proposals to desensitise the world to losses by eliminating recognition. People, animals, furniture, buildings—recognised or not. Without digital recognition, they simply didn't exist. The absence of items would not be questioned.

"You can't be here," said the woman.

"What? You're joking."

"No digital... you can't be here. Not recognised."

Anthea was angry. She had killed two people to get here. She wasn't leaving. And how was a Chinese woman running an Australian intelligence front desk anyway?

"Who are you? What is this place?" Anthea asked.

"Security and placement."

Placement. A new word for prison cells. Torture cells. Holding pens for people Ithica would later erase. Silent trials needed silent prisons.

Looking at the back wall—which hadn't existed a moment ago—Anthea now saw the outline of doors. Prisoners were being wheeled through, upright on trolleys. Strapped, chained, muzzled. Carried through a side door. Unconscious.

"I need to see your superior."

"There isn't one. I am superior."

Anthea knew not to make any sudden moves or she'd end up in placements immediately.

"I was ordered to come here by Pete Jacobs."

"I not know that."

"It should be in my file. Ordered back. Commanded. Pete Jacobs, head of Ithica."

"Nothing... no file," said the woman.

"Of course I've got a file. I've been working here twelve years."

"Building only been here eight months."

"I mean Ithica. Twelve years. Except I left two and a half years ago."

"Oh. That different."

"So there will be info on me."

"No. I tell you. You not recognised."

"I was commanded to return by Pete Jacobs."

"Yes of course... you stay here until a Pete Jacobs comes to collect you. I send you to placements."

"Callam Fairwither was sent to collect me by Pete Jacobs."

"Yes of course."

"You can look up Callam Fairwither."

"Yes of course... but no. FOI."

"FOI?" said Anthea, sick of hearing yes of course.

"Freedom of information," the woman replied smugly.

"Yes, I know what FOI is. Pete Jacobs needs to see me."

"Yes of course... but no. You don't exist. No digital."

Anthea recognised the stupidity loop. Designed to cover up necessary information. Callam should have warned her. He must have known what would happen the moment he sent her to the lift.

"How long have you been working here?" asked Anthea.

The woman hesitated. "Eight... eight days."

"Lucky. Probably longer than anyone before you," said Anthea, watching for a reaction.

"Why you say that?"

"I work in intelligence. I can see what's happening here. And what will happen to you. And the others before you. It's sad."

The woman looked uneasy.

"You're lucky so far. Or..." Anthea paused.

"Or what?"

"You have an extremely responsible job. There should be two people here doing what you're doing... but there isn't."

"I agree," said the woman.

"Most people in intelligence—especially in this building—work in secret. Don't appear on lists. You look for them... you can't find them.

It's not your fault. And they shouldn't blame you. But of course they do."

"They don't."

"Of course they do. And then they get rid of you. Make you not recognised."

The woman stared at her, alarmed.

"I came to Australia to escape," she whispered. "My father was murdered in the June Fourth Incident, Tiananmen Square. My mother was pregnant. She escaped Beijing to Harbin, then Russia, to Moscow. Many of her family were killed. I was called Xiaobao... Little Treasure. Came to Australia with help from Russian family I met in Kyiv."

"Kyiv, Ukraine?" asked Anthea.

"Yes."

"Who got you this job?" Anthea asked.

"Serge. My Russian friend. It is problem."

"It's not a good job... you could do a lot better," said Anthea.

"I think you're right. A lot happens here I don't like. Like saying you don't exist."

"But those are lies," Anthea whispered. "I do exist."

"I think you are correct," the woman whispered back. "It is like in China."

"For your own safety, you should leave," whispered Anthea.

"I feel that too. I will speak to Serge."

"If it were me, I'd leave as soon as I could. Like now," said Anthea.

Chapter 5
Coffee

Xiaobao had been kind enough to tell Anthea how to get into Ithica.

The lift ascended slowly. Too slowly. She wondered if Xiaobao had lied, or if she had trusted the wrong person again. Once inside, she would be directed to her workstation and pod. That was the promise.

When the lift doors opened, a thin, tidily dressed woman stood waiting. Her grey floral dress matched the space. Everything was light grey.

"Hello, you must be worried."

Anthea feigned a grin.

"Let's go and get you sorted out. Did you bring anything we need to get from your car?"

"No, no, definitely not," responded Anthea, remembering the dead body.

"You're not in Bay 42, are you?"

"No... where are we supposed to be?"

"Just checking," said the woman.

Anthea hurried to keep up.

"I'll show you your sleeping pod and work area. Both are on this level. Most people eat or have coffee breaks at the same time."

"I've forgotten your name," said Anthea.

"Not at all. You don't need to know. This is an intelligence agency, not a mothers' group... Oh—and we don't measure your weight anymore. Apparently even here people have rights."

"Really?" said Anthea.

"I know... I didn't believe it either. We were keeping people at their optimal weight. A couple of women were gaining weight, so their food intake was reduced, but their weight continued to increase... they were pregnant. I don't know how... and then they lost weight when they had a miscarriage."

"Really?... I mean of course. Of course," said Anthea.

It was a whirlwind tour ending with Anthea standing at a small desk surrounded by other women.

"One last thing. Do not go through that door. It's Pete Jacobs' office. I know you were Peter Jacobs' PA," said the meet-and-greet woman firmly.

"If you want to know anything, ask someone else. I've done this tour far too many times. Have a great day."

Briefly looking around, she counted seven women before looking at her desk with multiple screens. The woman to Anthea's right nodded, acknowledged her, then resumed being fixated. There were no windows. All had been boarded up.

Accessing her screens, Anthea was directed to an introductory presentation.

Immediately after this, Anthea created a duplicate workstation to ensure she wasn't being monitored. Now she could freely search for what was happening at Ithica.

It took minutes to understand why the tours never stopped.

Fifty-four women and five men had worked in the same office in the last six months. All had disappeared, but their wages and benefits continued. The workforce had supposedly grown by two hundred per cent.

Where was Callam, she wondered? Thoughts slipped through. She had become more depressed hiding in Carcoar. Her antidepressants had only lasted the first year.

After this Anthea experimented with alternative therapies. There were so many of them. She found herself doing yoga, meditation, eating saffron, and smelling lavender simultaneously. None of it worked.

Someone was there though. Someone was in her shed. She remembered the restraints, gagged then left. Coming to, there were packets of Panadol and several years' supply of antidepressants beside her bed.

Now concentrating on her screen, Anthea saw corruption had grown exponentially. The days of hesitancy were gone. Intelligence now had unbridled reign. More surprisingly were their paper trails. Where previously it was blatantly stupid for intelligence personnel to write anything except the absolute minimum, and even then in code, here were intelligence employees sending copious emails to each other, sometimes even private YouTubes.

Looking around at her work colleagues, they were studying and responding to their screens. All were busy doing different tasks, thinking the work was necessary. All were kept overly busy.

The few that did see what was happening were too afraid to speak up. Who could they tell? Their superiors were part of the corruption and disappearances.

Feeling thirsty, Anthea told the woman to her left, "I'm going to the kitchen."

The woman panicked. "It's too dangerous."

"I'll get a coffee from the machine in the hall," said Anthea.

"No, no... no. Don't go there. They..."

The woman hesitated, then whispered, "I'm Kate. We'll go downstairs. Three of us. It's safer."

"They...?" questioned Anthea.

The woman closed her screen and looked at another woman behind her.

"I'm not going down there ever again."

The other five women remained looking at their screens. Finally, one woman turned around to face Anthea and whispered, "I'll go."

The woman sitting to the right of her immediately grimaced.

"No, Anau," she whispered. "Think of us... I don't want you to go."

"It's only coffee."

"It's not. There's Cage."

"I'll be fine. Babe, I promise," said Anau.

Walking to the lift, Anthea looked across at Kate.

"Glad you're here... really," said Kate.

The lift came and all three silently got in. Heads down, knowing not to speak, waiting for the ground floor.

Anthea followed Kate and Anau to the coffee shop. Kate walked straight to the banquette seating in the front window.

Anthea immediately noticed the large number of sexy, masculine waiter staff. Far too many for a coffee shop. There were far too many baristas too. They looked more like runway models in their tight white T-shirts and tighter denim shorts. They were buff—thighs and pecs.

"Jespar will be with you soon, Kate," said one.

"Sorry you had to wait, babe. The usual?" said the waiter.

"Sure, Jespar," said Kate, returning his smile.

Like the other waiters, Jespar was using lines like, is there anything I can give you, and you take it easy, babe.

Walking away with their order, Jespar looked over his shoulder at Kate and winked before entering the kitchen.

This was Kate's cue to announce, "Do excuse me, going to the bathroom."

Anau said she was happy to go with Kate. Unsurprisingly, Kate insisted she go by herself.

Anau and Anthea looked at each other. Anau spoke first.

"I always get takeaway here. Kate and some of the others come here and..."

Anau was trying to work out what was happening. Some of the females were following waiters into the back of the café past the sign: MEN, FEMALE, SERVICES. It was unashamedly obvious.

"What's happening... How long do you think Kate will be?" asked Anau.

Anthea remained silent.

Women were now emerging from the corridor. Anthea had seldom seen women so happy coming back from restrooms. It was obvious the women were having sex with waiters. Less obvious if drugs were involved.

Anthea questioned if Anau was actually an intelligence analyst. She clearly wasn't comprehending what was happening.

Their two coffees were brought by another fabulously great-looking waiter. He held both coffees in his right hand and his left hand rested on the side of his crotch, further accentuating his obvious bulge.

"Will you be wanting anything else? Like..."

The word *like* hung in the air. The waiter winked at the same time. Anau was looking at the top of her cappuccino and missed everything.

"How long have you worked at Ithica?" asked Anthea.

"Melanie and I have been here three months now," said Anau.

"You're a couple?"

"Yes, and we have a seven-month-old son, Cage."

"Cage," repeated Anthea.

"We haven't seen him since we started working here," said Anau, producing photographs on her mobile.

"Cage... where does the name come from?" Anthea asked inquisitively.

"It was Melanie's father's initial surname," said Anau.

"Melanie's father was adopted?" asked Anthea.

"No, he changed his surname after the sex change."

Anthea wondered, but remained silent, knowing Anau would explain most things over time.

"At first only Melanie was being transferred to Ithica, but Melanie insisted we both get transferred," said Anau.

"And they agreed?" asked Anthea.

"Yes. We met three years earlier... and commenced living together almost immediately. We were both shocked when told we would be living in Ithica and no children were allowed."

"Really," said Anthea.

"A person at Ithica said they had specially arranged two women to look after Cage... It all happened quickly. We were driven out west to meet them one night. We had dinner and the two women played with Cage."

Anthea remained silent.

"Then they told us to leave Cage with Megan and Tiffany... that night... They said we had to... It was shocking."

Anthea was quietly horrified.

"I thought they were nice, but Melanie said she didn't think they'd been around children before. Melanie said it all seemed staged... Cage was happy though. They have a lovely house with a garden. There were toys everywhere... and that was weird, as there weren't any other children..."

"I'm sure there were," said Anthea.

"Melanie took it all badly and is still worried. She cries sometimes. She carried Cage... We've tried to visit Cage but so far have only seen him online."

Anthea took Anau's hand and reassured her. "I'm sure he's happy."

She then turned away from Anau and wiped the tear from her eye.

"A lot of people in our section seem to move on to other sections quickly, but you've both been there three months," said Anthea.

"Yes, we all worry about the movements. We were told it's important. Most of them go deep cover but they'll turn up again."

"Have you ever seen the people again?"

"No... not really... we've heard from a couple of them... they couldn't say where they were, or anything... it was good to know they're alive... Everything was fine."

Anthea was distraught. Anau seemed to fathom nothing.

"Was your father an intelligence officer?" asked Anthea.

"Yes, he was. Did you know him?"

"No, just a guess."

"You're good at working things out. I'm not," said Anau.

"That's not true, I'm sure."

"No, it is. I often can't see what's happening. Melanie tells me that all the time. She tries to explain things to me but I lose interest..."

"Does she tell you what she's working on... like now?"

"She did... it was after she climaxed yesterday... I forget now."

"Pillow talk," said Anthea.

"It's pretty bad when we both have sex and end up talking about work."

It was then Anthea saw Kate emerge from the corridor with Jespar.

Anthea smiled. Anau had no idea what was happening, and Kate was plainly hiding she'd just been fucked by Jespar.

"So sorry I was late, I just couldn't leave," said Kate.

"Before we go, what is so dangerous about the kitchen at Ithica or the coffee machine in the corridor?" asked Anthea.

Both Kate and Anau were hesitant to speak. Finally, Kate answered.

"I've been here a month. The only people here longer than me are Melanie and Anau. Some of the desks have new people each week."

"Carie's desk has two people per week. We haven't told Carie," remarked Anau.

"She's been here three days. It's when people go to the kitchen by themselves... We go in groups, it's safer," said Kate.

"The people who disappear. We're told they're all fine," added Anau.

"They're not fine, Anau," Kate said angrily.

Anau was surprised.

"And never go near Bay 42 in the basement," said Kate.

"No... there too," said Anau.

Anthea said nothing, now remembering the dead body still in the car boot.

"Bodies turn up there all the time," said Kate.

"More than 30 people have disappeared, Anau. They're not safe and alive," said Kate.

"Actually the number is fifty-nine in the last six months," added Anthea.

"Noooo," said Anau.

"I believe you," said Kate.

Anthea remained quiet going to the lift.

Arriving back, Melanie ran to Anau and hugged her. The two kissed before resuming work.

Returning to her desk, Anthea saw an envelope with her full name on it. It was an invitation from Pete Jacobs. It said tomorrow. After 10 am. His office.

Anthea sank into her chair. A meeting. Very formal. Anthea feared the worst. She escaped into her work. Australians fleeing Australia.

Military and intelligence families were selling up and moving to safer countries overseas. Moving quietly. Fearful of what was happening.

"To be expected," she said to herself.

All were afraid government authorities would confiscate their possessions.

Their safety net had disappeared.

Soon Anthea realised she needed to see Callam before meeting Pete Jacobs. Sending him a message, the response was immediate.

Phone number discontinued. Please try again.

Not being able to contact Callam wasn't unusual.

A message flashed up on her screen.

Superb security chief Xiaobao has been found dead in Ithica car park. If your car is in Bay 42 please organise cleaning.

"Bay 42 again," she mouthed.

When lunch arrived she took the paper bag and walked hurriedly to her sleeping pod. The pod was small and confined. Perfect for escape.

There were clean clothes neatly folded on the open shelves. Under the bed was another open space. Anthea crawled under and lay on her back.

Peace.

"Hello Anthea," said an unfamiliar voice.

Anthea looked around but saw no one.

Finally she noticed a pink dot pulsating on her computer screen.

"We haven't met but I have a message from Callam."

"You're a pink dot," said Anthea.

"No, I'm Shay," said the image now appearing on her screen.

The guy was naked and stunningly beautiful. More attractive than all of the waiters downstairs. Anthea wondered how he knew Callam and why.

"You're naked."

"Yes, Callam likes me naked."

Anthea could only think the guy is honest.

"He created me at SET 24. I'm his AI mentor," said Shay.

"Callam's still alive?"

"Yes. On another floor. Unreachable. I'm Callam's mentor."

"Well that's not working," said Anthea. "I need to see Callam. I'm meeting Pete Jacobs tomorrow."

"Callam knows," said Shay.

"How does he know?"

"I told him. You're to meet him tonight at Pythons. 9 pm."

"Pythons?" questioned Anthea.

"It's a gay pole-dancing club."

"Of course it is."

"Callam said to dress in men's clothing but don't stand out. Also it's Feather Boa night, not constrictor night, so no black leather—that includes shoes... And especially don't wear women's perfume. Gay men can tell immediately what you're wearing."

"I could wear drag."

"It's not drag night—that's every Thursday—and you'd look terrible in drag."

"So what should I wear, Shay? You're the mentor."

"Only for Callam. I'm his mentor. I help Callam as much as I can. I was created for SET 24. When Callam escaped, I survived too. I'm compatible with all technology. SND. Silent Non-Disruptive."

"You can go anywhere and not be detected?" enquired Anthea.

"Yes, but only on monitor screens. I'm not a 3D hologram. Much more flexible and faster, and I'm extremely efficient with energy. I'm not a guzzler."

Anthea looked at the naked man on her screen.

"Did he mention me?" asked Shay.

"No... never," said Anthea. "But I had scarce knowledge of SET 24. I knew it existed... I did see where it was set up to prolong the lives of human beings... and failed miserably. There was never mention of mentors," said Anthea.

"Navigating the world outside SET 24 took time to work out. I lost contact with Callam."

"But you're his mentor!" said Anthea.

"By the time I found him he'd managed to entangle himself in more trouble. This time far worse. I watched him for seven hours before determining how best to help him."

"Did he say where at Pythons?"

"No... but he'll find you."

Anthea was hesitant. She remained silent. Shay disappeared.

Elsewhere, Shay appeared on Callam's screen.

"You're here!" exclaimed Callam. "I'm so glad."

Shay now encompassed Callam's entire screen and asked, "Is that alright?"

"Of course it is, buddy."

The two looked at each other. Shay waited for Callam to speak first. Callam stared at Shay who moved his left buttock and repositioned his schlong so it now ran down his leg.

"They're going to kill me," said Callam.

"Again?" exclaimed Shay.

"No, for real."

Shay knew if Callam was killed by intelligence hierarchy then he would be terminated too.

"Seriously," added Callam. "But—"

Shay changed the subject.

"Are you looking at my butt?" said Shay, rubbing his hand against his firm buttocks.

Callam smiled.

"I was told to stay in my pod," said Callam.

Shay smiled and rubbed his hand slowly along the length of his schlong. "Really."

"You're supposed to be my mentor."

"Are you complaining?" said Shay, now rubbing his cock to erection.

"No, not at all," said Callam, while squeezing his left nipple.

"It's my job. I've got your back."

"Are we going to do this?" asked Callam.

"I'm here to please," said Shay.

Chapter 6
Pythons

Anthea looked at her naked body in the mirror. Of course she didn't like what she saw. How could she? The last years in hiding had been rough. Too rough.

Tomorrow she would meet Pete Jacobs in his office. How was this possible? Coming face to face with the very man who had tortured her and repeatedly tried to kill her.

She had to see Callam at Pythons. He would hopefully know what to do.

Flashbacks of previous experiences weren't helping. Too many questions never able to be answered. Over time the amount of corruption and evil at Ithica had grown exponentially. Fraudulent amounts once in their tens of thousands had become millions, and now billions.

Anthea's only defence was to immediately kill Jacobs. She knew he would pontificate about his leadership, diplomatically telling Anthea it was great to see her again, both knowing his ceaseless trail of corpses.

Failing that, she was lost. She now remembered she had also failed to siphon funds to escape Ithica. She had no excuse. It should have been her first priority. Callam would be reminding her. But you had all day, she could hear him saying. It was true.

She couldn't do it now. She had to start looking like a man. Not just any man. A gay man that no one would notice or recognise. And wear feather boas.

Anthea purchased a full body of men's shapewear. Her now non-existent breasts weren't a problem. She then cut her hair short, careful to look like a guy rather than an aggressive lesbian. A visit to the sex shop close to Pythons was now needed.

Just before 9 pm, Anthea stood in line with other guys to enter Pythons. She looked forward, not making eye contact, and trusted her large-framed rose-tinted glasses were sufficient. There was no security guard, just a man in a hole in the wall wanting payment. Anthea handed money over and moved forward to the club. Through a corridor and around a corner, two doors later she was in.

She now saw herself in a mirror. She could never get used to looking like this. Like a man. A costume change and suddenly she had more power.

"Almost believable. Thank God it's dark," she muttered.

Looking around at the other guys there, she saw she blended in.

Another guy wearing only a long black feather boa asked Anthea if she wanted to cloak anything. Looking down at the guy, she felt unsure and responded no.

"Don't worry. If you change your mind just come back, darling."

Darling. Anthea was initially worried she must still look like a woman. She was wearing an easy-squeezy soft-pack six-inch soft cock. The bulge was evident and obvious.

It was only when the cloak guy called another guy darling Anthea relaxed. The guy was wearing a sexy black leather harness and a black feather boa protruded from his firm arse cheeks. She remembered being told it wasn't leather constrictor night and was surprised when another leather-clad guy ran up and hugged him. At the same time he slowly pulled his feather boa from his arse. Four yards later the boa tail was wrapped around them both.

Walking forward, Anthea navigated another wall of mirrors. Her first thoughts were of the carnival hall of mirrors she'd visited as a child. Then there were dark corridors opening to spaces with male pole dancers and crowds of men. How would she ever find Callam, or he find her? She'd rung his phone but no answer.

Leaning against a corridor wall watching a pole dancer, a muscular waiter asked if she wanted a drink. Anthea recognised the guy from the coffee shop that morning. Wearing only a swimmer, she could see why women kept going back.

"A gin and soda," she said.

Anthea realised the waiter couldn't hear her. The guy leaned closer so she could speak in his ear.

"A gin and soda, thanks."

Anthea likewise put her ear towards his mouth. "Stay here, I'll come for you," he said, licking Anthea's ear with his tongue. It felt like a lingering kiss.

Waiting for him to return, Anthea recognised people she knew from Ithica and elsewhere. A married judge was talking to a young male recruit from Ithica. The two were groping each other, oblivious to the other men around them, the judge fondling the young man's groin.

Anthea knew the judge's wife and their two young adopted children. The judge's wife was trapped in the marriage, threatened if she did try to leave the other judges would destroy her completely in their judgements. She would get nothing and lose all access to her children.

Some judges purposely married women from overseas so they could send them back if they got tired of them or changed their mind. Particular police would help judges with false charges and false police reports. In the worst cases the woman was sentenced to jail then sent back to their country of origin upon release.

Gay, bisexual and curious, Anthea learnt early many of the people working for intelligence were ambivalent with their sexual tastes. They simply wanted satisfaction from whoever. Sometimes whatever when it came to toys. Anthea had tried to remain heterosexual but it was a lonely gig.

She was now hesitant to stay for the waiter's return. Hopefully Callam would walk by. She had to see him tonight. Anthea then thought he might already be dead.

The waiter returned.

Anthea said, "No."

She continued, "I mean yes."

While paying for her drink she tried to explain. The waiter smiled, winked, nodded, and left. She was alone again, free to explore.

She worked out there were three different areas where pole dancers performed. Then there were the dark corridors, labyrinths of mirrors, darkened seating areas, and the list went on. Anthea identified a place she thought most people walked by and sat in a darkened area, careful people wouldn't recognise her. It was spook stuff 101.

She was pleased with the vantage point until moments later a good-looking guy in his twenties asked if he could also sit down next to her. Anthea reluctantly obliged, saying she was waiting for someone.

The two watched the guys walk by and smiled.

"You're Anthea. You work at Ithica. My brother used to talk about you," the guy whispered into Anthea's ear.

"Who?" said Anthea, trying to deny it.

"I love the pink glasses."

"Who?" Anthea repeated, now wondering who his brother is.

"Christian Duffley."

Anthea smiled. It was the wrong thing to do.

"I'm sorry to hear that," she said loudly, almost yelling.

"Are you Timothy or Alex?"

"Alex is my sister."

"Fair call. I heard about your brother. And your father."

Anthea was lying. She'd watched the video of Christian being tortured and killed during his initiation. Forcibly recruited into intelligence. Their father was originally told Christian's death was an accident. Asking to see his son's body—more lies. Christian had been burned and disposed of with the other recruits that day. It wasn't a one-off occurrence.

Their father threatened to go to the media and police. Consequently their father was drugged and sent to a psychiatric centre. After this the family was told their father disappeared. He was killed in the psychiatric centre. Once again military and government officials got rid of whoever was in their way.

"The whole thing is horrible," she Anthea.

"I complained, wrote to everyone I could, saw my local member of parliament. Total waste of time. All I got were threats. They said they'd jail me for five years," said Timothy.

"You need to be careful. They're not joking," said Anthea.

Anthea attempted to change the subject. They'd both been watching the stream of guys going past but no Callam. There was nothing Anthea could say that would help Timothy. Australian Defence and intelligence kill their own.

"I'll see you around, Christian. I mean Timothy, sorry," Anthea said, still thinking about Christian's torture. Timothy and Alex didn't know what really happened. How terrible it all was and is.

Wandering through another section of Pythons, Anthea found a bar.

"A gin and soda," she said to the bartender.

"And how's your night going?" the bartender replied back.

"I'm looking for a guy."

"Me too. Do you know the guy's name or you got a photo, not that he'll look like his photo? You mightn't even have his real name."

"Callam."

"There's a lot of Callams on Grindr at the moment. Do you have a photo?"

"I don't know him from Grindr. I just know him."

"OK. So his real name."

"What's he look like?"

"In here he looks less than average. Brown hair," said Anthea.

"Has he got a job?"

"Works for government," Anthea said, trying to remain non-specific.

"Callam from Ithica."

"What?"

"Callam. Works for Ithica. Spy agency."

"You have spies in here?" Anthea said, acting surprised.

"Honey, don't pretend. You're not good at it. This place is crawling with your mates. We don't mind. You spend a fortune here and we don't ask where your money comes from."

Anthea remained quiet. Intelligence personnel weren't supposed to splash their stolen cash for all to see. Their lifestyles, including assets, had to remain secretive.

"Commanders, we've got generals, supreme court judges, high court judges, prime ministers, billionaires, royalty. They all come here because they know our guys stay mum. And our security is better than yours any day. We identify everyone who comes here through airport security recognition. One up on you guys," said the barman.

Anthea was curious. She'd recognised one judge so far and a couple of people from intelligence. This was their safe place. A dark gay nightclub.

"I know what you're thinking. We've got a private backroom section," added the bartender. "And three back doors to it."

"I need to go there."

"No you don't. If they want you there they'll get you."

"I work for intelligence."

"You think we didn't know that when you walked in here?"

"I'll get the police to raid this joint."

"Federal or state?"

"I'll get both," said Anthea.

"Then you'll need to speak to Paddy and Patrick. They're here. We call them Paddy Fits Patrick. It's a dad joke. You get it. Paddy works state. Patrick's federal. Paddy's trying to get into federal through Patrick."

"I get it," said Anthea, feeling frustrated.

"But you'd know all this being in intelligence. And they're here three, four times each week. We had a queen from Montenegro meet his king here, and a whole army of others."

"I need to see Callam. It's urgent."

"Well if Callam thinks it's urgent he'll see you."

"He told me to come here. It's more urgent than he thinks."

"OK, I'll let him know it's super urgent."

"They're going to kill me tomorrow," said Anthea, realising she was now yelling at the barman.

"And why are they waiting?"

Anthea tried to compose herself.

"Have your gin and soda, honey. Relax. This isn't a drama bar. Have a look around. Take a seat. Our cameras show where you are. We track you. We can find you. I'll tell Callam."

"You track everyone in here?"

"Yeah, welcome to real intelligence."

The corridors of mirrors to the different stage areas were dimly lit. Anthea watched guys walking through, some hung out in corners waiting and hoping, others were blatantly fucking. She appreciated their winks, nods, and opening lines as she walked through. They were all friendly, glancing around at each other, acknowledging each other or lost in happiness.

Anthea sat at a table in one of the darkened edges of the spotlit stage. She was soon joined by three other guys; all knew each other. Acknowledging Anthea and thinking she was a guy, the guys continued talking amongst themselves. Anthea watched the male pole dancer.

"Pete Jacobs is here," said one of the three guys.

"Fuck no."

"One of the waiters warned me he's roaming around," said the tallest of the three, Brock. Anthea recognised him from Ithica.

"Where?"

"Think about it, Lyle. Roaming around means roaming around."

Anthea could see the three guys staring at each other, worried and looking confused. Brock had survived being tortured. She'd seen his whole terrible session. Somehow physically he'd recovered but mentally he was a ticking time bomb trying not to be cruel like his torturers. Brock had his arms around one of the guys sitting on a stool.

"We should get out of here, Brock," said his partner.

"I know, Andy, but I'm trying to get better. My counsellor said I should confront my problems."

"She didn't say start with Mt Everest," said Andy.

"No, I'm not saying you're wrong, babe. And I realise I'd be dead if it wasn't for you."

"I want to go, for your sake."

"There's no point leaving now," said Lyle. "He's here. Whoever he's after."

"I know, I know," said Brock.

"Jacobs is here for a reason. Someone's going to die. Maybe me. Someone. Or several people," said Lyle.

Anthea instantly thought that person was her.

"Lyle, shut up. You really are too much," said Andy.

Anthea was meeting Jacobs tomorrow. Was he stalking her? Perhaps he'd kill her tonight at Pythons. He might be the last person she ever sees?

Why wasn't Callam here now? She needed him now. He must know she was at Pythons. Why wasn't he meeting her?

By now Brock and Andy had left in one direction and Lyle wandered off following a guy who had walked past. It was frustrating but all she could do was wait for Callam. Once again, she wondered if all of this was a set up to kill her.

She should leave like Brock and Andy. She assumed they were leaving. It made sense until she saw them sitting at another table on the other side of the stage.

Suddenly a slim guy with a ballet dancer's body had wrapped himself around the pole on stage. An announcement said his name was Liam. Anthea thought he was stunning, in little time shedding his clothing piece by piece.

"You want a great top?" said Liam, then tossing his singlet to a sexy guy sitting at a table near her.

His butt-hugging shorts were the next to go.

Liam now threw his underwear directly at Anthea's face. Recovering, Anthea saw he was now only wearing a shimmering G-string. She couldn't help but notice his bulge. His cock was moving around in his loose-fitting pouch.

The guy seemed to smile directly at Anthea, and wink. He moved his tongue around his lips while looking directly at her. Swinging around the pole he would again stop immediately when facing her. Members of the audience were throwing money at him on stage.

"Strip, strip, strip. Show us. Show us," the audience shouted. Liam was fabulously pirouetting on stage before hurling himself back onto the pole spread-eagle into a reverse grab spin. His strong legs open in front of her. Anthea recognised some of the other positions from her school days, particularly the Ayesha twisted grip. She'd never been able to do the complex moves but took classes to watch the other guys. Liam was again pirouetting and threw off his G-string. The crowd went wild now seeing Liam's prominent cock. Anthea looked hard every time Liam swung around. Guys were clapping in beat to the music. Others throwing more money. More guys were now naked, dancing and cavorting. Suddenly the music stopped and Liam did the splits immediately in front of her.

She looked at Liam smiling at her. Besotted, she couldn't stop looking at him. His cock was pointing directly at her. Next she knew they were face to face.

"Callam said to come get you," Liam said, regaining his breath.

"Who?" said Anthea. She couldn't understand how she was so attracted to the guy. Yes, he looked perfect. He looked like a Greek god. It was too dangerous. The timing was wrong. She was about to be killed. That's why she was at Pythons. And then the reality. She was disguised as a guy.

"Did he tell you my name?"

"No, he pointed to you on the monitor and said to get you. We need to go."

Anthea was hesitant. Everything was happening at once. Love. Death. It was a trap. Callam wasn't here.

"We have to go," he said. "Trust me. I'm taking you to Callam."

Anthea froze. Trust me. He'd said trust me. Every time a person had told her "trust me" it had resulted in lies, attempts on her life. Or like now, she was about to be killed.

Following Liam through the club Anthea stared at Liam's every movement. She wanted to reach out and touch his firm buns. She may as well.

He took her hand while opening a concealed doorway to lift doors.

"It's a security check. You have to be hanging onto an employee's hand in order for the door to open. Otherwise an alarm goes off."

"Does it have to be your hand?" she said, looking at his schlong.

She was trying to hide feeling terrified. More so now. She was leaving crowds of people behind. Her experience with lifts was not good.

"Hang around and find out," said Liam, smiling. "We'll go to level four."

Stepping out of the lift, Liam stopped suddenly to check there was no one in the hall. Anthea ran into Liam, who steadied her. The two looked into each other's eyes. Liam gave her a light kiss on the lips.

He didn't know, was Anthea's immediate thought. He didn't know she was female.

Liam dragged Anthea to the end room. The door said Luxe Penthouse.

"We're on the top floor?" questioned Anthea, wanting to know when she escaped in the future.

"No. There's three floors above, why?"

"Just the sign says."

"It's like a test. If clients ask is it really a penthouse, we have to pleasure them more so they don't care where they are, or what they're doing."

"That's true."

"It can be," said Liam, winking at Anthea.

Anthea looked down again at naked Liam. She felt slightly younger. The childish jokes of sexual innuendo they shared. She'd seen other children do it when she was younger. Often though she was the centre of the joke. Sometimes her care families were laughing at her survival. It seemed they didn't care. Perhaps they didn't.

More PDST. She remembered an asthma attack. As a child she always carried her Ventolin spray. Often a spare Ventolin too. To most people it was a cold night. Her care family had insisted they all go camping in the woods.

Her care father telling her, "You can't be sick all the time. You have to take chances. Your asthma isn't bad."

Anthea had used her Ventolin puffer before she went to sleep. Waking up in the middle of the night she needed more. This time someone had put powder in the top of her puffer. It went down her throat and her breathing passage.

She immediately reached for water and her spare. It too was full of powder. Having another asthma attack, the next thing she knew, bright torches were shining in her face. She was the centre of their joke. Anthea spent the rest of the night outside near a creek wrapped in her sleeping bag, struggling to breathe.

She tried to work out who she was afraid of more. The living or the dead. Her care family seemed to know nothing about care.

Now standing in the penthouse, Anthea and Liam could now hear voices in the hallway. Liam instinctively told her to get under a covered dining table near a bathroom. He would greet them.

"Which room do you want?" asked Justice Jack Bastian, opening the penthouse door.

Anthea could hear the conversation. She recognised Judge Bastian's voice.

"Jack, I brought three guys. I thought we'd share them, like," said Justice Dugal Leech.

Both Jack and Dugal now saw Liam in the room.

"Liam, you're here," said Jack. "His Honour, Dugal Leech, who you know very well, was attempting to explain to me the benefits of sharing guys. He knows, and you know, Liam, I refuse to share guys."

"You may have mentioned it," said Liam. At the same time he glanced back to see Anthea was hidden.

"I know I hate sharing," said Jack.

"I love sharing," said Dougal Leech. "Sharing out peoples fortunes... or misfortunes. That's why I was promoted. I have no problems breaking up families, separating children, making sure legal teams get very well paid, of course. Leaving people so poor there's no way they can appeal. I have the lowest appeal rate of all the family court judges in the state."

"I need to take a shit instead of listening to yours," said Jack Bastian.

Wandering to the bathroom Jack fell firmly onto the toilet seat.

Liam looked again where Anthea was hiding. The judges were drunk. They might easily bump into where she was hiding.

"Divorce shouldn't be available to everyone. The sooner people realise they'd be financially better off if they don't divorce. Just put up with it and shut up," said Dugal.

"You're joking of course, Dugal," said Jack.

"No I'm not. You know I'm not," said Justice Dugal, now standing in the bathroom and taking his cock out.

"I need a piss," said Dugal, pointing his cock first at Jack before swinging around to the vanity basin.

"And an accountant. Someone said you have one. I have some money that's not showing up anywhere. Need to move it," said Dugal.

"How much?" asked Jack, watching Dugal in a mirror pee into the vanity.

"Hundreds. More," said Dugal.

"Thousands."

"Millions," said Dugal.

Anthea heard the conversation and was surprised.

"A hundred million? How'd you get a hundred million," asked Jack.

"Mainly a lot of drug dealer syndicate divorces. They don't want the wife or anybody to know how much they've got. And the tax department watches these things. They need a judge they can rely on, sort it out for them."

The two looked at each other. Jack was struggling to get off the toilet.

"Guys, can you help His Honour get off," said Dugal.

"They don't have to call me Your Honour."

"It's showing respect," said Dugal.

The three guys attempted to lift Jack off the toilet. Liam stood back ready to help when needed or direct them away from Anthea.

"I didn't know how much I was fucked downstairs," said Jack, being lifted onto a chaise.

"We're not going home yet," said Dugal.

"I have a silent case judgement to hand down tomorrow morning," said Jack.

"For Defence?" asked Dugal.

"No Intelligence," responded Jack.

Anthea wondered who they were putting away this time.

"Is it difficult, hiding people in Australian jails?" asked Dugal.

"No, of course not. No. No. They're already in jail. I hand over the judgement and it remains classified. They tell me what the judgement is," said Jack.

"Who's they?" asked Dugal. "Or shouldn't I ask?"

"It's security classified. Doesn't matter though. One of the attorneys in Defence Legal or Intelligence Legal. The person in the case tomorrow threatened to go to the media. He has files. We raided his house. So we're putting him in jail. He's had enough warnings."

"Did you find any files when you raided his house?" asked Dugal.

"No, but didn't really expect to," said Jack. "So they planted files. They're security classified and can't form part of discovery. It's a silent trial anyway."

"And intelligence quietly pay you for it?" said Dugal.

"Of course. Defence pays less than Intelligence though. Defence says they have trouble hiding all the siphoned money they give us," said Jack.

"My arse," said Dugal.

"They gave me an Order of Australia last year. After I demanded it," said Jack. "Frankly I'd rather have money any day."

Liam interrupted, "Guys, before we get you comfortable and we make you really happy, let's move you into the Palace suite of rooms."

"Where?" asked Jack.

"The rooms with the spas, steam room and slings," said Liam.

"Why didn't we go there in the first place. Why are we here?" asked Dugal.

The three guys were soon carrying Jack and Dugal to the Palace suite. It was one floor above. Jack was wheeled out of the room on a chaise. Liam locked the door as soon as they left.

"You heard them," Anthea said as Liam helped her get out from under the table.

The two of them stood up next to each other. She was dressed. He was naked. Anthea looked at his eyes. They were crystal clear. Nothing in her life was clear. She looked down and stared at his hardened cock.

"Have you eaten?" he asked.

She was more confused now.

"I was thinking of Callam. He should be here," she said.

"He's in the club. He knows you're here," said Liam.

Liam directed Anthea onto an oversized sofa.

"It's large. Everything in here is large," Anthea said before looking at Liam's cock again. Now swelling more. Liam moved closer to her.

"You are so wonderful," she said, but worried any minute Liam would find her easy-squeezy soft-pack six-inch soft cock.

"Callam said I should look after you. Make sure you're happy. Not notice penthouse doors," Liam said, attempting to unbutton Anthea's jeans.

"No, not yet. As much as I want to."

"I understand, don't worry," said Liam.

"You must see, have sex with a lot of guys. Good, great-looking guys. Some of them."

"It's my job, I need the money," said Liam. "But when guys know I work here. It's not good, they leave me alone. I prefer women."

Anthea was confused but smiled. "Really? Like really?"

Anthea questioned what was happening. Had Liam just said he prefers women.

"Yeah, totally," said Liam.

"I don't think you can say totally."

Liam kissed Anthea again.

"You're working in an all-male sex club," she said.

"You're sweet," said Liam.

Anthea tried to work out what was happening. Did he know? Did Liam really prefer women? Was he just saying it to make her comfortable, thinking she was male? Perhaps Liam did have sex with men to survive but preferred women. Was he living a double life? Was she overthinking it? He was certainly bisexual. No, she only knew him to be gay.

Both Anthea and Liam were surprised when Callam entered the room.

"Oh no. You're here. I mean... why now?" said Anthea.

"I locked the door," exclaimed Liam.

"So what?" said Callam, walking over to them.

"Callam, Pete Jacobs is going to kill me tomorrow," said Anthea.

"I know."

"And kill you and everyone at Ithica."

"Yes."

"And Jacobs is here tonight."

"I was trying to get her to relax," said Liam.

> Anthea immediately stopped talking. Liam had kissed her.
> He was hard. Was it all pretence.

"You're stressed. I was going to give you a massage."

"I knew that. I did."

"We need to go," said Callam. "Liam, put some clothes on."

Chapter 7
Silent Trials

Resplendent, wearing only a golden towel revealing everything, Justice Jack Bastian is wheeled on a chaise out of the lift along the hallway to the Palace suite. Dancers run ahead to open the double marble doors, where more gorgeous buffed men meet them inside. Jack hears flourishes of flutes, horns, and bells foretelling his arrival and looks at Dugal walking by his side.

"This is what opening court should be like every day," said Dugal.

"It's hard to do this for secret trials," said Jack.

"No, no, no... the military has all their pageantry, the public never sees... We need more pomp. Wigs and robes aren't enough now."

"What do you mean now... Dugal?"

"Judges have more power now... we have more control... secret trials sending people to jail... asylums... having people killed... Australia doesn't need a death penalty. We kill whoever anyway."

"You're a family court judge... You don't kill people," said Jack.

"Yes I do... and can," said Dugal.

"What?"

"I do... and I keep an eye on all my cases. I map them out."

"Mapping what... you're not making sense," said Jack.

"When I give a judgement I monitor how long until the husband commits suicide, breaks the law, loses his job, falls behind in maintenance, goes bankrupt. Sometimes I go after the woman, and don't get me started on gay marriages."

"What?" repeated Jack.

"I set one party up to fail, sometimes both."

"You don't," said Jack.

"Yes I do. It's easy, family court is forensic and secretive. The family court doesn't use clients' real names in their judgements. Legal teams intrude into their lives to learn everything they can, and charge for it... I can do whatever I like... varying degrees of severity in judgements get various results. Suicide or murdering their ex and children getting top points... Severe judgements have severe consequences... I can give you examples."

Jack looked at Dugal. He was grinning, pleased he could destroy people's lives.

"There was a case last year. Arub Lienstein, his own manufacturing business."

"Dugal. I don't want to hear."

"He's married six years, three young kids in private schools, large mortgage. Wife wanted a divorce 'because she's not seeing enough of him."

"I wonder why?" said Jack.

"The legal team, her barrister, I let them destroy her husband completely. I knew James, her barrister, from law school. The defendant lost his business. My judgement... wife and children got everything. There was no appeal. Made sure he couldn't afford it. I expect Arub to commit suicide in three to six months according to my stats. Bankruptcy isn't going to help him. I pulled a few strings. Made sure he lost his jobs in the last four months. He's going to try and steal something and the police are arranging that."

"Dugal, you can't destroy people in the family court. Other courts yes. Don't you feel anything?"

"No... I'm sick of helping people. And have compassion. Compassion. When I started as a judge I'd occasionally help people. But a couple of years later the same people turn up with the same problems. That's why I keep records. My previous judgements weren't harsh enough. I look now at what breaks people. And give it to them."

"But on average people get married three times in this country. You shouldn't be doing this."

"Other judges follow my decisions. I'm setting a standard."

"You're talking about precedent law?" said Jack.

"Yes."

"But we both know that doesn't work. You look for the precedents to suit your judgement with no regard as to what really happened in the court case," said Jack.

"Totally... The drug lords pay me to deliver. I couldn't survive as a judge without them. You're the same with your secret trials."

"Secret trials are far more severe."

Their procession at Pythons had stopped and both men now realised there were at least twenty beautiful men around them.

"Where are the showers? I want a shower," said Dugal.

Hearing this, six guys showed Dugal through a bedroom and into a large wet area filled with wall and ceiling water jets. Dugal didn't hesitate, lying on a central raised platform where the guys gathered to wash him. Jack watched Dugal being entertained sexually and bathed. Jack could smell the pitchers of scented oils poured on his body, then rubbed in.

Still reclining on his chaise, Jack looked for Liam but couldn't see him. He hoped he'd show up soon. Until then, he'd enjoy the other guys around him. Looking across into another bedroom, he saw what he took to be an Alaskan king-size bed. He'd spent three days in Palm Springs in an Alaskan. It was supposed to be a judicial conference. It was certainly judicious—being sensible and well-judged to hold the conference in gay mecca.

He would have more sex, another drink, and go home. The males around him moved him into the Alaskan and continued arousing him. All quiet. It was pleasurable. Jack was thinking of tomorrow when the guy closest to him said something.

"You look worried," the young guy said, touching Jack's chest.

Jack looked at the guy and briefly wished he was him. He hadn't really noticed the guys playing with him.

Alabaster white skin, smooth, chiselled, his voice was crisp, sparkling, and so sexy. Jack held his hand out to touch him. The guy moved closer so Jack could reach wherever he wanted. He hadn't noticed or seen the guy before. Jack thought he was gorgeous.

"And what do you do with yourself?" asked Jack.

"Whatever you'd like," the young man responded.

"No, seriously... I'm interested."

The young man smiled but didn't answer the question.

"What's your name?" Jack whispered in the guy's ear, as if the two were alone.

"You'll only forget it," the guy responded.

"That's not true at all... You're an artwork."

The guy laughed and laughed more. "And this is your pitch to guys?"

"No... no... it's not... I never ask names... I'm surprised I've asked yours."

"Well perhaps you shouldn't have."

"Are you twisting my words... toying with me?" asked Jack.

"I think you're the one toying. I've seen you here before... I know you don't ask names."

"How do you know that?"

"We know who we're entertaining. Your inclinations, preferences. What gets you on heat."

"And what are mine?"

"You really want me to tell you?" said the young guy.

"I think so."

"You usually come here with the same 'friends'. Spend time with them. They play together. You separate. Your preference is being fucked, and leaving. Always alone. You don't ask guys their names nor ages. You're not interested. You're single. We're not told what you do but told it pays well. You have a preferred whiskey. You don't like people."

Jack rolled his eyes at the guy and waved his hand, indicating the other men go.

"But I like you. You're not people."

The guy leaned forward to kiss Jack. Kissing became fondling, became uncontrolled sex. Both came once, Jack then trying again to cum, bringing back his youth, before falling flat on the bed.

"What's your name?" Jack asked again looking at the guy on top of him.

"I told you."

Jack wondered if the guy would tell him now.

"You don't ask names," said the guy.

"But I'm asking yours."

"Laddy."

Jack stared up at the ceiling. He could see Laddy in the ceiling mirrors and watched him roll over onto his back and lie next to him.

"You look worried again," said Laddy.

"I am, but you're not supposed to tell me."

"Why?"

"Surely here, of all places, they tell you not to ask people their problems."

"No, I mean why are you worried?" said Laddy.

"I don't want to say."

"I told you my name, Laddy."

"Is that your real name or your—?"

"It's my real actual name, I'm being honest with you. Real."

"Well I wish I could be real with you. By the time you get to my age nothing is real."

"So you're an assassin," Laddy exclaimed, trying to bring levity to their conversation.

Jack laughed. "I guess I am. I'm a judge for silent trials. The kind you never hear about."

"I was joking," said Laddy.

"You should judge your audience better."

"In Australia—you're a judge in Australia?" asked Laddy.

"Yes."

"But that's not very democratic."

"Correct."

"What do you have to do?"

Jack was still feeling ecstatic after sex with Laddy. He realised this was pillow talk, but he needed to talk to someone.

"It's going to be a tough couple of weeks. Defence, Intelligence, the Governor-General, PM's department. All keep piling on the work. Each year there's a need for more and more secrecy. They call it security. That's why I come to Pythons. To escape the world."

"Along with all the others escaping... So what's so bad this week?"

"I will have to have sex again with you if I tell you," said Jack.

"It's possible."

"I want more sex with you, Laddy."

"The same," said Laddy, now playing with Jack's chest hair and nipples.

"First up tomorrow I've got a list of defence personnel I'm supposed to incarcerate."

"Why?"

"Differing reasons. Some know too much and hierarchy's afraid they'll talk. Usually they just kill them and take their possessions. There's a lot of theft to deal with. Not just weapons and ammunition but rocket launchers, armed military drones. Public never hears.'

Laddy remained poker faced.

"Occasionally a case appears in the public court system so people see the system works. But if it goes off the rails, the case disappears. Media's told to shut up."

"I always thought the media gets it wrong," said Laddy.

"Solicitors are told not to put their head up and help. It's obvious to them now. Otherwise, they'll be sent to jail instead of their client."

"That's terrible."

"Intelligence is a dirty and disgusting mob. They get away with everything. I think they kill more of their own than Defence. They're all human fodder."

"I had no idea?"

"No one does. You don't see it. I don't either. I'm told what their judgements are and what they've supposedly done. Sign off. I have no idea. Otherwise I'll join them."

Laddy snuggled in closer to Jack.

"Are you afraid you'll be killed?" he asked.

"No... I know I'll be killed. Especially with what's happening now."

Laddy continued to listen.

"Some judges have died in the last couple of days. It might be coincidental. But there's other things as well," said Jack, turning his head away from Laddy before looking back.

"Are you safe?"

Jack didn't respond.

"Intelligence is killing off another agency. More people will disappear. Other agencies have gone."

"Kill them?" questioned Laddy.

"Yes..."

"Why?"

"Whole heap of reasons. Huge amounts of money syphoned from projects. Secrecy. Stolen documents sold overseas to countries or companies. Murders in the agency. Sometimes the agency's a sham anyway. When you've got secret projects and no accountability people do what they like. And now secret trials... You probably think I'm mad?"

"No... No... Complicated," said Laddy.

Jack smiled.

Laddy remained quiet. He could see Jack was greatly upset.

"The people on the intelligence lists are the worst off though. They're forced to work for the agencies. All are Australia's brightest. They're isolated from their families and friends. No regular contact. Out of sight, out of mind. They disappear easily."

"You can stay with me tonight if you like. Here. It'll be safer," said Laddy.

Jack kissed Laddy again.

"Well I can't go home."

Justice Moran Morus flung open the doors of the Palace suite and tried to make his appearance known. Jack heard Moran's obvious voice.

"Guess who?" Jack whispered to Laddy.

"He's bad news. He might be a judge but he's a bigger idiot," responded Laddy.

"You know he's a judge?"

"He tells everyone. I guess it's because it's impossible to believe. And he's a sleazeball. He treats us really badly."

"I know," said Jack.

Moran opened the doors to their bedroom and remained standing. His rotund body tied up with two leather harnesses, body fat obscuring parts of the harnesses.

"You didn't wait for me," Morus exclaimed to Jack.

"When?"

"Monday night... No Tuesday... maybe Wednesday."

"Today's Thursday. You're speeding."

"I've got six cases over a year old to make judgements on. I'm trying to do them."

"You get your associate to write them. You just have to read them. We all know that."

"I need more time. What if they make mistakes? I know it doesn't matter. There's appeals. I don't like them. I know the other judges protect me with appeals, but, but. It makes me look stupid... Who's that?"

"It's Laddy."

"How do you know his name? You never ask names. Whenever I ask you who a guy is you say you don't know."

Jack looked at Laddy and winked. "I don't."

"Well you send him away. I need to talk to you. Can he disappear?"

"What's so important?" asked Jack.

Jack was irate Moran thought he could always order people around. He knew Moran often found out what was going on before other judges. He was a gossip monger, often wrong, confusing the names of people and what happened. Most people didn't discover this early enough though. It was therefore necessary his associate wrote his judgements. The Chief Justice had even said it was imperative.

It was another instance of justice must be seen to be done, even if the person supposedly doing it wasn't the person doing it at all.

"He needs to go," said Moran.

"He's not moving off my chest. I like his hard cock. What is more important?"

"It's important. It's private," said Moran.

"Nothing is private with you. You tell everyone everything in your usual muddle."

"Yes but I'm correct."

"Seriously. You're seldom correct, and don't let me remind you how you became a judge."

"Autumn's invited me to her house for dinner tomorrow," said Moran, trying to change topics and sound impressive.

Unbeknown to Moran, Jack had been invited too, along with others. The invitation had preoccupied Jack's mind all day. Nothing good would come from seeing Autumn again.

And then there was Anthea. Jack knew Callam was specifically sent to bring Anthea back. Jack had discovered from Callam a couple of people at Ithica had known where Anthea was hiding the whole time. They had told no one. Monitoring her, Pete Jacobs particularly had watched Anthea suffer with worsening depression, panic attacks, and poverty whilst she hid under a dilapidated shed.

Those who knew her plight refused to help, worried for their own safety. Pete Jacobs had made it known he wanted Anthea to suffer and go mad.

Chapter 8
Her Morning After

The fire door at Pythons was difficult to open. Anthea thought it was locked at first. When it did creak open, Anthea, Callam and Liam tripped down two stairs into the pitch-dark alley.

They fell together. Liam was immediately on his feet. Anthea noticed because, in his haste to leave, Liam had wrapped only a feather boa around his waist, and it was now against her face. That, and his appendage, which Anthea presumed had become excited by feathers. She felt her left shoulder was injured from falling but remained quiet. It was blindingly dark and impossible to see other people in the alley. She sensed most were men making out, more than in Pythons.

In complete darkness, Anthea was lifted by two muscular arms she assumed belonged to Liam. Standing on her feet, she was sure it was Liam. It felt like Liam.

"Where's Callam?" she questioned.

"He was behind us. I think he fell on me, jumped up and disappeared."

Anthea called Callam's name several times.

"We should go to Spits," said Liam. "Callam will meet us there."

"It's an all-night diner," added Liam. "Around the corner."

"Hang on," said Liam, moving slowly through and around groups of people.

Anthea could feel some people standing, others on their knees or bent over. Someone shot water into her eyes. Wiping it away. It felt more like gel. They were incrementally moving towards the end of the alley.

Liam had placed her hand on his cock and repeated, "Hang on."

It seemed like the longest time Anthea had ever stood in line for anything. When Liam discovered her name... rejection, acceptance, indifference. It was Liam's call. Then it hit her. Her life was over. His was beginning. And why had Callam insisted she dress like a guy and meet him at Pythons? Why had she agreed? She felt so vulnerable. Willing to do anything. And why was she still hanging on to Liam's cock? She wasn't letting go.

"Anthea," a voice said. "Anthea." It was Callam, immediately beside her.

Liam turned around, recognising Callam's voice.

"Good, you two stayed together," said Callam.

"Spits," said Liam.

"Spits," replied Callam.

The street was dimly lit, not pitch black like the alley. Anthea could now see the sign "Spits", lit in changing gay rainbow colours.

"Did you see Pete Jacobs tonight?" Callam asked Liam.

"Luckily no, but people told me he was there."

"I thought it best we leave," said Callam. "I'll tell you why at Spits."

"Why is the diner called Spits?" asked Anthea.

Anthea saw Callam and Liam look at each other and smile. She immediately thought it must be a gay thing.

"They got the sign wrong. It's supposed to say Spitz," Liam said after hesitation.

Anthea sensed she wasn't getting the true answer.

Walking into the diner, Anthea immediately noticed it was brightly lit. The waitress was staring at near-naked Liam.

"Don't worry, honey. I know it's feather boa night. And try to take it home this time."

"Thanks, Rachel," said Liam.

"We've got enough Pythons stuff to open our own fetish shop," Rachel said, looking at Anthea. "You guys having the usual?"

"Thanks, Rachel," said Callam.

"And your friend?"

"Just black coffee, no milk," said Anthea.

All three were now sitting in banquette seating.

"I'm seeing Pete Jacobs tomorrow," said Anthea.

"I know. That's why we left Pythons," said Callam.

"He's going to kill me," said Anthea.

"No Anthea, he won't," said Callam.

"You said yes before."

"Well, he won't," said Callam.

"Guys," said Liam. "You call him Anthea."

"He is," said Callam, now seeing Anthea frown.

"It's my name," said Anthea, trying to take charge. "I needed to see Callam tonight. He told me to dress like a man and meet him at Pythons. None of this makes sense. And my name is Anthea, and I'm not gay, but working at Ithica I may as well be."

"I don't get it," said Liam. "I hear they kill people at Ithica... all the time. You work for them?"

"Yes... " said Anthea.

Callam nonchalantly rolled his eyes and pursed his lips at the same time.

"I know what goes on at Ithica, ASIO, Signals Directorate," said Anthea. "We've lost a lot of colleagues, Callam."

"The guys at Ithica... we're told they move on. Like Sean Davies," said Liam.

Callam nodded.

"Yes," said Anthea, frowning.

"Norbert... he was fun. He wanted to leave Ithica but couldn't. He vanished... but we got an email from him saying he was fine and life was good," said Liam.

"Pack of lies," said Callam. "I remember Norbert. Short curly black hair, wore round green reading glasses, smart, never had a bad word for anyone," said Callam.

"Yes, and huge wide cock," added Liam.

"He was tortured and died during initiation, covered up, classified," said Callam.

"He told us he'd gone back to the Netherlands to live," said Liam.

"No, he was added to the list of tortured intelligence recruits," said Anthea.

"But how is it kept silent?" asked Liam.

"It's not silent. A lot of people know. Intelligence and military hierarchy, those present during the torture, from Prime Ministers down, Defence ministers, judges... the torturers themselves," said Callam.

"I sat in on a trial a few years ago. The judge asked if particular people were dead and listed on the Australian intelligence recruits torture list," said Anthea. "It didn't surprise them. The judge knew about the list. Didn't express concern, nor say this shouldn't happen," added Anthea.

"Jimmy Sitwell is incarcerated in a mental asylum, never to be released," said Callam.

"There's a bucket list of ways intelligence agents are killed," said Anthea.

Callam remained quiet.

"Sent on a secret mission they can't possibly return from, deadly car accidents, staging suicide is the easiest, died in hospitals, friendly fire, military accidents, disappear, no questions asked or answered, alcoholism is easy, organised drug overdoses, diving accidents, then there's the slow ways—induced cancer so the agent dies slowly, induced strokes," said Anthea.

"Must keep intelligence really busy?" questioned Liam.

"These are all quiet methods. It's not like spy novels or movies where half the town or planet is destroyed," said Anthea.

"It's all done quietly, none of the big war stuff where dozens of people are killed. Whole freeways destroyed. Buildings blown up," said Callam.

"Oscar, he was really nice," said Liam.

"Oscar Weiss?" asked Callam.

"Yes."

"He was financially helping his poor parents in Perth," said Liam.

"Disappeared," said Callam. "And a senior intelligence analyst stole Oscar's estate. His parents got nothing."

"It's horrific. You're dead the day you join," said Anthea.

"Surely someone can try to expose what's happening," said Liam.

"Those people are dead," said Callam.

"Defence and intelligence spend most of their money on expensive acquisitions, not disclosing actual costs, not on personnel. A lot is siphoned. Politicians fear they'll be destroyed if they say anything. At worst you'll have a military government. You could say we have that now, when heads of military become Governor-Generals," said Anthea.

"That's happened... hasn't it?" asked Liam.

Callam nodded.

"Callam, you loved Norbert. One night I was pole dancing and Norbert joined me on stage. We had sex on the pole. Best time. You watched. You could have joined us. I can't believe he was killed," said Liam.

"I wanted him, but he preferred you," said Callam.

"Yes, but I'm not gay," said Liam.

"You told him every time. I know," said Callam.

"Norbert gave me money up front to pay my rent for a year. Who does that?" said Liam.

"Norbert loved you," said Callam.

"I know, and I loved him."

"And a few others," added Callam.

"It's my job. And I think I'm good... at... entertaining."

"You're great at it. Fools me every time," said Callam.

"That's not fair. I'm not fooling you, Callam. When I'm with you, I so enjoy being with you. I try to make you feel terrific... because you are... I love being with you," said Liam.

"You love who you're doing," said Callam.

"Yes... if you want to be blunt. I have to be careful though. Some guys get jealous or vengeful," said Liam.

"Norbert wasn't like that," said Callam.

"No... we had fun... and he told me I was more available than you. He said he'd tried to see you but you were always doing something else... working."

Anthea watched Callam remain quiet, thinking.

"Norbert said that?" asked Callam.

"Yes," said Liam.

"And I told you. I said Norbert wanted to see more of you. He loved you. He wanted to be with you. Preferring to see you... I was a fill-in. He was waiting for you," said Liam.

Callam glanced at his watch. "I have to go," he said, rising from the table. Retrieving money from his pocket, he placed it in front of Liam.

"Make sure Anthea gets home safely," said Callam, looking at Liam, then rushing out.

"But—" said Anthea.

"You'll be fine tomorrow with Jacobs..." said Callam.

Anthea and Liam watched. Callam didn't look back.

Anthea looked at Liam. He was trying to be stoic, but a tear was running down his face. She waited for him to say anything.

"Never, never... I never thought... Norbert and the others were murdered. Like... all of them. It's serial killing?" asked Liam.

Anthea held out her hand. It was there if Liam wanted to hold it. Liam took a napkin and wiped tears from his face.

"I remember my cousin. She'd been raped by a police officer and his mate. She reported it. Nothing. She said most people never see justice. I guess that's the same here... I don't know how you keep going, Anthea."

Anthea remained quiet. He'd said her name for the first time.

"Let's go home. You can sleep at my place. Spare room," said Liam.

Anthea looked at him. She was hesitant, but she wanted to.

"Just knowing someone else is there tonight will help," added Liam.

The walk to Liam's apartment took ten minutes. Anthea was surprised how ritzy the building was. Doorman and twenty-four-hour concierge. It was luxurious. The doorman recognised and acknowledged Liam, who seemed oblivious he was wearing only the feather boa.

"Norbert paid you a year's rent here?"

"Yeah, and he got the place for me. I was in a studio... some of the clients at Pythons are really generous. They say they'd rather give it to me than their wives. At least they get happiness from me, they say."

Anthea was confused. For a guy calling himself straight, his definition was very broad. So far he might be bisexual, but not hearing about any of his sexual pursuits with women, he seemed to be exclusively gay.

Entering his apartment only reinforced this. Two large statues of well-endowed naked Roman men stood side by side in the living room.

"I had a gay interior designer do the styling for me. He said I needed the two large naked male statues to bring out the feminine side of the interior. He said having one Greek column was male, having two Greek columns is female. Same for statues."

"All I see is two large erect marble cocks. Are they the columns he was referring to?"

"I guess so," said Liam. "I'll open some wine."

"I'll find the bathroom," said Anthea, taking the opportunity to finally look like a woman again. Lipstick, powder and hair cream.

Anthea settled into an oversized velvet sofa opposite two marble studs. Liam returned and nestled next to her. She hoped he had noticed her attempt at femininity.

"Wait, wait," Liam exclaimed, jumping up from the sofa and running down a hall.

Anthea watched him jump up, his firm buttocks poking out before he took off. She wondered what he was doing. He soon returned and nestled in again, this time wearing a pair of light blue silk shorts and a matching silk T-shirt. Touching them, Anthea thought they were so thin and delicate. Like butterfly wings.

"Sorry, I was wearing my work clothes," said Liam.

Looking at him, his outfit hid nothing. His broad shoulders, guns, nipples. Anthea looked at Liam closely. Blue sparkling eyes. He was adorable.

"You still think I'm gay?" Liam said, looking at Anthea.

"It's easy to get that impression. Performing at Pythons. Knowing some... a lot, of the guys you've had sex with."

"It's the money. You can see it pays well. I'm really not gay."

Anthea remained quiet.

"A mate got me the job. Taught me everything. How to identify first what's the guy's biggest turn-ons are. Then have the guy shoot his biggest load ever... though my preference is women," said Liam, now running his hands and tongue over Anthea.

Anthea was still quiet.

"But that's not easy."

Anthea laughed, then smiled.

"You look more beautiful as a woman," said Liam, kissing her.

"I didn't look too good as a guy," said Anthea.

"I thought you were gender-transitioning."

"What?" Anthea said, putting her head back.

"No. No... not at all. And why does it matter? My preference is older women."

Anthea was still confused.

"One at a time?" questioned Anthea.

"Yes, one at a time. Are you always this difficult? I'm trying to say I like you. I'm choosy when it comes to my partners. And it's not been the easiest of days. You're probably used to it."

"No... yes... no. It's numbing."

"Yes... It is," said Liam.

Liam leaned forward to kiss Anthea. Anthea responded, hugging Liam. Simultaneously, Liam reached down for Anthea's cunt. Anthea didn't hesitate and reached for Liam's cock.

"I read sex can help you get through difficult and depressing times," said Liam.

It was a night Anthea would remember for the rest of her life. She became euphoric, seeking out more and more sex with Liam, and he the same with her. Each increasingly pleasuring the other. Somewhere between night becoming day, each was naked, twisted around the other. They had passed out together.

Waking up with Liam, Anthea thought about it and remained still. She felt perfect. Everything felt perfect. Staring up at the high ceiling, she could see a mirror positioned showing her and Liam lying naked together, her hand on his genitals. Anthea stared at the mirror. Was she the happiest she'd been in her life? It felt like it. Looking across the room, somehow one of the marble statues had fallen backwards. She didn't remember that at all.

Then it hit her. Thirty-eight and he was twenty-three. She'd told him she was thirty-eight. She'd had sex with a male god. No wonder she felt terrific. He'd made her feel awesome, even invincible. She knew by the time she returned to Ithica she'd be feeling fearful, depressed and worried. The ultimate high gone. But that was her life. It wasn't perfect. There wasn't anything good about it at all.

Thinking she knew what was to come. Her thoughts about suicide. Of course, lately it was different. She was killing people. Anthea was sure if she thought about it long enough it would make sense. She had to tell Liam she didn't want to see him ever again. Of course it was a lie.

She didn't want to make him feel bad, though. He had made a good life for himself having sex with men despite saying he preferred women.

Right now wasn't the time. Liam had manoeuvred around and was now licking her clitoris really well. She would wait. She began thinking about the day ahead at Ithica and her meeting with Pete Jacobs.

"Do you know where I am, honey? Why don't you reach out and take what you want," said Liam.

Anthea waited until Liam ejaculated in her before telling him she didn't want to see him ever again. It seemed like the right thing to do. He was young, beautiful, sexy. It wouldn't work. Liam protested.

"I have my work," Anthea exclaimed.

"What work? I've never heard Callam or Ithica do anything except help spies, judges and politicians get away with murder and fraud all the time. It's got nothing to do with intelligence."

Anthea quickly dressed. She walked to the front door, turned to look at Liam still lying naked on the sofa, and walked out quietly, closing the door behind her.

"I've forgotten something," she exclaimed.

Chapter 9
Passageways

Returning to Ithica, Anthea wondered why no-one asked where she'd been. Perhaps she was being monitored. Settling into her desk, she sensed the office mood. Something was wrong.

"She's gone," Kate whispered to Anthea.

"Who?" Anthea mouthed back.

"Anau... they say it's suicide."

"But she's got Melanie... and Cage."

"Cage is missing..."

"He's seven months old."

"There's no record of him ever existing."

"There has to be... I'll look."

"I've looked. We've all looked. Melanie's been sedated."

Anthea turned to search on her computer. Medical records of the child, birth certificate. Nothing. All were gone. Facebook, Instagram, other social media posts—removed. It was a lot of effort to remove Cage's existence. But why?

Anthea remembered other intelligence families were often threatened. Forcibly recruited into intelligence, agencies thought they owned the agent and their family. Some agents were forced to have abortions. Sometimes agents and their partners were killed. Anthea remembered two gay agents in 2006, in a relationship at the time. Anthea instantly remembered other examples.

"Adoptions," said Kate. "To a diplomatic family being transferred overseas."

"But Cage is seven months old," said Anthea.

"By the time he reaches two, he won't remember his original parents. By five they'll be gone."

Anthea realised it was true. And Melanie and Anau would probably be dead by the time Cage reached five.

"Cage mightn't show up in adoption records yet. The system's slow," said Anthea.

"His name, age and birthday would be changed."

"Giving Cage to Australian diplomats going overseas makes sense. Looks more like a family rather than two spies acting as diplomats."

"Adoption numbers in Australia are low. Two hundred and fifty in the whole country last year. It's impossible to adopt here," said Kate.

"If he's abducted by diplomats, he'll be forcibly recruited into intelligence in his twenties," said Anthea.

"We can't check his DNA. It's all eradicated. I think Cage is gone," said Kate.

Both women stared at each other, then turned to face their computers. Anthea could see Kate wiping away a tear from her eye. She was doing the same.

Trying to change the subject, Anthea asked Kate if she had seen Pete Jacobs.

"Why?" asked Kate.

"I'm supposed to see him today."

"We never see him. How many times has he wandered through here? That door to his office—I've never seen anyone use it," said Kate.

"He's called me to a meeting today."

"But I was told you're arch enemies."

Anthea, Kate and the others watched as their monitor screens all froze.

"There, it's happened again," Kate whispered to Anthea.

"What?"

"The monitors freeze, then the computers die and eventually restart... The person who's disappeared... their computer is usually the last to commence. Haven't you noticed?"

"No," said Anthea.

"It's like a moment's silence," said someone in the background.

All remained silent while wondering which would be the last computer to restart. They anticipated Anau's. Anthea was hoping it wouldn't be hers. One woman reached for a flask in her jacket, popped the top and hurriedly drank the contents. Whatever it was, she fell forward and collapsed on her desk. The others remained silent and still in fear.

Anthea knew she would have to kill Pete Jacobs. She was more determined to kill Jacobs now. Even if she failed, she had tried. Others saw what was happening but had done nothing, expecting others to step in and do what needed to be done. This was their modus operandi their entire lives—pretending to see nothing, then doing nothing. The result: afraid they would be next to disappear.

Her computer screen started. Looking around, two computers were yet to commence. She thought to herself she was safe... for a brief moment.

Strangely, Anau's computer had restarted. Two computers hadn't, though. One person burst into tears while clutching her chair; the other ran screaming from the room.

With her computer working, Anthea quickly resumed creating her nest egg on her undetectable login account. Could she escape? It seemed impossible. She then crossed over to her allocated account. There was a note from Pete Jacobs.

"You are commanded to meet me at 1900 hours. Tap twice on my office door then enter, follow directions through corridor. Do not turn back. Tell no one about this message."

It was 1812 hours. Anthea prepared herself for the meeting. It would be a battle. Win or die. She knew if she was injured she would have to take her own life rather than face a slow death. Anthea steeled her mind.

Leaving her desk, she went to her pod, prayed to God for strength. Her relationship with God had always been tenuous. She then went to

Jacobs's door. She was about to face her nemesis. If people in the office were watching, she wasn't aware. She was focused. Her life and theirs were at stake.

Knocking twice, Anthea waited before opening.

"Do not turn back," Anthea mouthed to herself. It was the words Jacobs had used commanding her to the meeting.

Opening the door, Anthea saw a corridor. She remembered reading, follow directions through corridor. What directions?

Then, as if on cue, a white mist swept along the floor from the end of the corridor towards Anthea. It seemed innocent enough. No—perhaps it was poisonous, or there would be more to come engulfing the entire space. More fear.

Either she was meeting Pete Jacobs or her whole trip had been a trap. Anthea walked through the mist without stopping. It felt cold around her legs. At the end of the corridor was a thinner passageway. She took it. By now she was feeling slightly dizzy and frustrated. Up ahead was a man lying on the floor. It looked like Pete Jacobs. Approaching, she saw it was a mannequin.

"Have you nothing better to do?" voiced Anthea, walking past the dummy.

Feeling more light-headed, she continued on. Finally, there was another door. Opening it, Anthea was blasted by more mist. Through the mist she saw Pete Jacobs sitting at an oversized desk.

His head was down reading, he raised his right hand, indicating she should stop. Anthea looked at Pete Jacobs and waited. She knew she would have to get closer if she was to kill him.

"Hello Anthea, did you have a good journey from Carcoar?" Pete Jacobs said, looking up after several minutes.

"Yes, Sir, thank you."

"No speeding fines, accidents, murders, dead judges?"

"No, Sir, country life is very uneventful."

"Good to hear. And you had no problems with security?" Jacobs said, now standing in front of his desk.

"None I can remember, Sir," said Anthea, feeling confused. She couldn't remember seeing him move. She was feeling more dizzy. The mist was affecting her.

"We've moved since you firebombed your last office. Unfortunate, but it had to be done. I learn you've settled in well here. Taken up with a gay sex worker."

"It's good to be back in Sydney, Sir."

"Call me Pete. I've always had a fondness for you, Anthea."

"It's never been apparent, Sir."

Anthea wondered what was happening. Pete Jacobs was now standing in front of a fireplace she hadn't noticed before.

"How are your parents?" asked Pete Jacobs.

"They're both dead, Sir, but thank you for asking."

"I'm glad you like your new office space. I understand it's open plan. We're having trouble retaining people," said Pete Jacobs, now standing behind her.

Anthea turned around to face him.

"I would love to discuss retention rates with you, Sir."

"That would be great, Anthea," said Pete Jacobs, now sitting on a sofa.

"We have a problem with retention rates," said Anthea.

"I totally agree," said Pete. "I'm fed up. We give them the best training, no expense spared, we look after them—housing, food. It costs a fortune. And then..."

"What, Sir?" Anthea asked, walking toward the sofa, hoping to get closer to Pete Jacobs.

"They disappear or commit suicide," Pete Jacobs said, now standing.

Feeling faint, Anthea sat on a chair.

"Worse still, go to work for overseas agencies," said Pete. "They're a disgrace to Australian intelligence."

"I don't know of any agents who have gone to overseas intelligence agencies, Sir."

"Well, you wouldn't, Anthea. And it's not because you're a woman. I just wonder what we're doing wrong. I think we're forcing unsuitable people to join intelligence in this country. We threaten them to join, telling them we'll ruin their lives if they don't. And they screw up. The others, who apply to join though—they're staying. We have a recruitment department for a reason. So it looks like we recruit people normally rather than forcibly," said Jacobs.

"Was there anything specific you wanted to tell me, Sir?" asked Anthea, trying to stay conscious, knowing she would need an opportunity to kill Pete Jacobs.

"Good question," said Pete Jacobs. "I wanted to thank you for coming back to Sydney. I'm told you're fitting in. The other thing—the reason I called you—Ithica is doing well. We're pleased. But at the same time, I'm informed Ithica, and all the people at Ithica, are going to be got rid of."

Anthea remained silent, trying to watch Pete Jacobs's next move.

"I think the best thing you can do is kill yourself now. From what I've seen it's quite easy. I've left an L-Pill on the desk and a suicide note from you."

"I think I'll decline, Sir."

"This isn't my decision, but if it is, I'm sorry," added Pete Jacobs.

"I thought we were going to talk about retention," questioned Anthea.

"We are," said Pete Jacobs, now turning away from Anthea. It was Anthea's chance. She could hardly see him through the mist, but he was visible. She rose from her chair, walking quickly, then pounced.

Coming to, leaning up against a corridor wall, Anthea tried to remember what happened. Her head was aching, and feeling her forehead, a large lump had formed.

There had been the meeting with Pete Jacobs. Yes, maybe no. Anthea wondered if she met him or imagined she met him. He told her to kill herself. Sounds as if they did meet.

Had she been drugged? Why—how was she still alive?

Thinking back to years earlier, he seemed different now. Previously he was shouting, yelling for things to be done. This time he'd been placid. No regret. Matter-of-factly.

She wondered how much time was left. Her plans for revenge were failing.

She wasn't going to take her own life. If Ithica was obliterated, she wouldn't need to kill herself. Her frustration was building. Sitting in the corridor was like sitting in a trench. She'd been there before.

The little games she had played to stay alive, cope with her sad life, put up with everything being thrown at her.

Her thoughts turned to Liam. The highs and the very lows. Remembering last night. It had been perfect.

It served no useful purpose to tell her work colleagues they were about to be killed. Anthea smeared her lipstick across her face. It was a subtle pink but effective enough for her colleagues to notice it was smeared. They would jump to the wrong conclusions and ask the wrong questions. Distraction.

Managing to get up onto her feet, Anthea hesitated before opening the door, breathing in and out quickly, as if she'd been running, exercising, or engaging in sex. She opened the door and waited for their reactions.

Chapter 10
Glass Chairs

Society brothel madam Autumn looked into her gilded mirror. Gritting her teeth, she watched her cosmetic stylist.

"Hair, make-up, hair, more hair. Susie. You're fiddling. I'm not a mannequin," Autumn protested.

"No, you're agitated."

"I am not... and if I am... and I'm not."

"Autumn, you've been in this state for two days."

"Now I'm in a state."

"You know you are... I don't know why."

Susie remained quiet, waiting for Autumn to apologise.

Autumn sighed. "I'm sorry, and I'm glad... you told me. I thought I was hiding it."

"From me. Ha, ha. What's wrong? Is it health?" asked Susie.

"No, no... it's judges. I'm trying to get them all in a row."

"They'll be in hiding... thinking they're next to be murdered... with good reason..."

"Their deaths aren't random. Something's happening. I've invited a few tonight. And there are other things they're doing wrong."

"You ordered them?" questioned Susie.

"Careful... OK, ordered. Judges become a gaggle of geese when you put them together. Each trying to assert authority over the others. Gossip, gossip. A pecking order. Who's the loudest... and when... and all the money I pay them... they'll be screeching."

Autumn and Susie looked at each other in the mirror.

"Will you be alright?"

"It's a lovely shade of eyeshadow," said Autumn, raising her eyebrows and changing the subject.

Autumn couldn't remember how long Susie had been her stylist. They had become friends. In time, Susie had moved into Autumn's overly large residence.

"What time are they arriving?" asked Susie.

"One's already here. Noll Moneytree, head of Treasury. He brought his latest twink with him. Some newly arrived gay Russian porn star refugee... I can't stand Noll. Total user, playing with other people's money. Treasury will be picking up the bill for the Russian. They wanted a bedroom. I put them in the garden shed where the dogs sleep. The Russian kept saying thank you. Generous host, in Russian. Well, that's what I'm told he said."

"Is the Russian handsome?" asked Susie.

"No. No way. I'm not putting another gay twink on the payroll."

"I wasn't asking."

"You are. He can go work at Pythons."

"You know he can't. They have a no-Russian policy. Not even vodka."

"I invited Noll's wife too. It should be interesting."

"She just became a family court judge. Madelaine Dumbly."

"Yes, another family court judge with the perfect family. Deluded wife, gay husband and his gay lover."

"Why invite her?"

"She handles family court cases for intelligence personnel. She's on the payroll. Though for how long, I don't know."

Autumn and Susie smiled at each other.

The noise was loud. An explosion. No. It came from the front of the house. Susie quickly turned on the security images. An oversized ute had rammed itself into the front garage. It looked like a ram raid, with debris everywhere.

A smaller screen now focused on the driver.

"Jack Bastian announcing his arrival," said Autumn to Susie.

Autumn calmly called her residence manager, Toby, and told him to drag the car and driver out of sight down into the garage.

"Like last time," responded Toby.

"One of your judges?" asked Susie.

"Jack Bastian, alcoholic, depressed, naturally bi-polar, probably driving without a licence. The media covers it up, the judges say nothing."

Autumn and Susie watched as Jack fell out of the passenger side onto the driveway. He soon jumped to his feet and looked towards Toby.

"Toby, I'm a judge," he could be heard saying. "Say nothing. Don't tell Autumn. I owe you one."

"Why's he driving that large black ute? It's totally too big for him," questioned Susie. "He's got a Commonwealth driver."

"It's going to be a long night if I don't take control of them. I'd better go down," said Autumn, adjusting her pearl necklace, then standing and waiting for Susie to kiss her on the cheek.

"Stay here and watch their antics on security screens if you like. Josie can bring you dinner."

"I know. As long as you're fine, I don't want to know why judges are being murdered. I'm sure there's a million reasons."

"You're right," said Autumn, leaving the room. Walking down the corridor, she continued thinking of the many questions needing answers. Her guests all had their own agendas. The deaths of their colleagues had scared some of them. None had heard the full number. More judges would be killed or vanish. Distressing. She'd come to rely on them, to blindly do what she wanted.

"I don't want you to get it wrong like last time. Appeals cost money," she had said, chastising a newly appointed judge.

In one recent incident, a former barrister had been promoted after selling out a client. Not being able to discipline judges, his promotion to the bench was necessarily instantaneous. It saved him and a few other judges further investigation.

Until now, Autumn had always felt comfortable in her home. It had been her fortress, but tonight was the exception. She had to entertain tonight's invited rabble. She had counted them as friends—no longer. Turning a corner and reaching the balustrade, Autumn for once took hold of it.

Would she and her guests tonight all be killed?

She had said it aloud and quickly checked no one was around. Like the other killings, there were no warnings, no trails. Just cold murders disguised as mishaps, accidents, end-of-life events.

Walking down the stairs, Autumn felt destined to be another perfect murder.

"Hopefully not tonight though," she said to herself. She was concentrating, but she could only do so much. She had to control her guests. The last three weeks had gone horribly.

Reaching the bottom of the stairs, Autumn knew she wasn't concentrating as she walked through the gallery hall.

If only Justices Paramount, Bacon and Smatliefer were the only judges dead. She'd heard of three others disappearing and two judges who had supposedly quickly retired, their whereabouts unknown. Autumn saw the media was now keeping quiet on the murders and disappearances.

What wasn't she seeing? Thinking further, there were no real connections or relationships between any of the missing and deceased judges. Yes, they'd all thrown cases. She was fortunate the new anti-corruption administrator was more corrupt than any of them. He was there to save them and himself from investigations.

And the people trying to kill her. She was seventy-two. She'd survived so far. She had lost some friends. That was horrible. Was it really? People and possessions had come and gone. Autumn couldn't work out which she missed more. She knew she was supposed to think she missed people more than possessions. But was that really true? It wasn't her large house that wanted her dead. It was some of the people she'd invited.

Rising from the chair, Autumn quietly opened her living room door. No one noticed her entry. The guests had settled into three groups around the room. The exception was Judge Madelaine Dumbly, who had isolated herself on an overly large chesterfield in the middle of the room. No one was going near her.

Judge Jack Bastian was sipping coffee and sitting with Nicholas Poulus and Barry Porfellow, who was Minister for Defence, at the far end of the room.

Phillip Nobetter and Neander Goot were huddled in front of a large fireplace off to Autumn's left. They were both occupied studying an obscurely lit young naked man lying in the fireplace, masturbating.

Doing a headcount, there were eight instead of ten. Noll Moneytree was still in the shed. Pete Jacobs hadn't arrived.

Autumn nodded to acknowledge Chief Justice Abraham Lylieberman, who was closest to the door and had visited her brothel the previous day.

"Abraham, it's good you came."

"Was there an option?"

"You had a three-hour freebie yesterday with two of my girls."

"We've lost three of our judges. It looks like we'll lose more. Am I right?" whispered Abraham to Autumn. "I could be next."

"So could I, good dear friend," Autumn quickly replied, while taking a folded piece of paper from her pocket and placing it in the palm of Abraham's hand. "I've written a short list of outcomes for upcoming cases requiring new judges."

"Thank you for your efficiency, Autumn. It's overwhelming."

"I can write their judgements as well."

"Once again, you're too kind. Definitely not. We're all worried by what is happening. Police said they can't guarantee our safety if we turn up for funerals."

"I've never known police to be able to guarantee anything."

Autumn was now looking at Justice Dugal Leech, who was carefully studying a painting on the wall.

"Dugal had just left Justice Barry Paramount's home that morning," said Justice Abraham Lylieberman looking directly at Autumn before staring at Dougal. "And now Barry's dead."

"Seriously," questioned Autumn. "Is that right Dugal, you were the last person to see Barry Paramount, alive?"

Dugal remained looking at a painting on the wall.

"You saw Barry Paramount?" asked Autumn raising her voice slightly.

"What?" was Dugal's response. "I know the people who used to own this painting."

Autumn didn't like where this discussion was going.

"It was stolen from their house along with a couple of others," said Dugal.

"I've had this for as long as I want to remember," replied Autumn. "You should remember Dugal, I've given you two paintings. One was a Streeton. "

"Autumn, I had lunch with the PM yesterday," interrupted Chief Justice Abraham Lylieberman.

"About?" asked Autumn bluntly. She was secretly annoyed. She had made it her business to know who PM's and others were meeting privately, secretly and sexually.

"The PM was asking for a favour. I knew I should run it by you first though. Get your advice," said Abraham.

"If it's the PM, it can't be that urgent. It can wait until tomorrow."

"Totally," said Abraham.

Autumn now saw two of her maids bring in a tray of Veuve and commence distributing among her guests. She watched as Madelaine Dumbly refused. Even when it was explained it was a toast to the dead judges.

Madelaine saw Autumn looking at her.

"Yeah, you look at me. Toast. Toast to your death Autumn." said Madelaine in a rage.

She was swinging her hands in the air.

"You people made me a judge... To have me killed. I know my husband organised it to get me out of the way. Make me a family court judge. Pathetic. The people in my court shouldn't have been allowed to get married, let alone have children. And they want me to sort out their their family problems. Half of them aren't related to the people they think they are anyway. It's true. Why? So they can do it again and repeat. They've never been able to sort anything in their lives. And I have to show understanding. It's impossible. How can I show them understanding when they've never properly understood anything anyway? They shouldn't be allowed in a court building, any court building."

"It's a toast, Madelaine, to our three friends who have passed," said Autumn, making sure everyone in the room could hear.

"Well, I didn't know them."

"Yes, you did. You knew them very well. You used their judgements and wisdom as precedents while studying law, in your cases as a barrister, and you'll continue to do that as a judge," said Chief Justice Abraham Lylieberman.

"No, I don't. I use the precedents I want to use to make my point. If litigants don't like them, they can appeal. You guys cover for me. It didn't take me long to learn that."

Others stayed quiet. As much as possible, judges had tried to cover for each other. Many judgements were dependent on appeals to achieve justice, giving solicitors and barristers greater opportunity to make money.

"I'm informed it's time for dinner," said Autumn, "and to take the opportunity to show you my recent extension."

"More?" questioned Nicholas.

"I purchased the house next door."

"The one you've already built under? Did they find out?"

"No, not that one, the other side, Nicholas," said Autumn.

Nicholas was all excited, and more so when the walls either side of the fireplace began to move down to reveal a dark, cavernous secret passage.

"The underworld," said Nicholas.

"I seriously hope not, Nicholas," said Autumn.

Like an excited school child, Nicholas ventured into the dark passage first.

"It's a lot colder. I can hear water," he said.

All was black. Nicholas followed light patches down a wide ramp to a huge open floor below.

The others followed behind Nicholas, chasing their own coloured spotlit areas on the floor until they were walking down a ramp.

Her guests were used to Autumn's theatrics, and soon they were all standing in the same dimly lit area. Black curtains rose, revealing a large space seemingly built under two houses.

An overly large round table and ten clear glass chairs were then lit in golden light. Surrounding the table, fit young naked athletic guys were dancing provocatively with each other. Other men were hanging from ropes swinging through the space.

Her guests moved to surround the table.

"I wish our three colleagues were alive to see this," said Abraham Lylieberman.

"I do too, Abraham. Nigel used to love watching naked men perform for him."

"Too many things are going wrong. We need to sit down and talk," added Abraham.

"Yes, we do," said Autumn.

"I want to join the dancers," said Nicholas.

"We need to sit, Nicholas," Autumn said sternly.

"Sit down," Autumn added, looking directly at Nicholas, then looking around at the others.

"Where? There's no place cards," questioned Phillip Nobetter.

Autumn looked at Nicholas and the others sternly.

"Sit."

All found chairs very quickly.

Scantily clad male waiters rushed in to provide guests with their favourite cocktails and sex toys.

Nicholas sat to Autumn's left. Madelaine sat two chairs away. Phillip Nobetter tried to sit as far from Madelaine as he could, but it had been a scramble for seats. He was the newest judge, but already well aware of Madelaine's dramatic antics.

Autumn smiled, watching her guests take their seats and, more obviously, not sit next to Madelaine, leaving vacant chairs on either side of her.

Her guests were attempting to get comfortable. It was difficult. Autumn watched them squirm. The clear glass chairs were cold, with raised ripple lines making them difficult to sit on.

Knowing her guests would be unable to get comfortable, Autumn watched as they quietly talked to each other.

Four huge screens now dropped from the ceiling.

"It's another Roman Bacchanalia," said Chief Justice Lylieberman.

"No, this isn't a Bacchanalia," Autumn said clearly, her voice now coming through the sound system. She was the only one standing.

"I've always done my best to look after all of you. My little dinner parties. Gifts, jewellery, artwork, some say stolen. The girls... and guys have entertained you at my brothel and home for years. They are my family, and I liked to think you are too."

Abraham tried to speak.

"No, Abraham. I have tried my best to add happiness to your lives. We have gone through some hard times together. Now I find all of you here... want me dead and gone."

Several shook their heads and muttered no. Barry Porfellow, Minister for Defence, was the only one to speak.

"That's not entirely true, Autumn."

"Barry, you have done more back-stabbing than anyone here. What are you saying? And why use the words 'not entirely'?"

"We're restructuring Defence. Changes."

"You're getting rid of another intelligence agency. This time, Ithica."

"That might happen."

"It already is. It's like the BJORN project."

"There's no need to get into specifics. It's historical."

"Barry's right, BJORN is historical," added Chief Justice Abraham Lylieberman.

"BJORN isn't historical. The government's still paying money for it. I supposedly have a cleaning contract with BJORN," said Autumn.

"Well, you're the last person who should be talking about it," said Barry Porfellow. "Just take the money."

"And now it's Ithica. Judges associated with Ithica are being killed," said Judge Neander Goot.

"We have a legal system and justice for all in this country," said Barry Porfellow.

"You're joking, aren't you?" said Dugal Leech.

"So what does Ithica actually do?" asked Justice Neander Goot.

"Jack... you should have a go at this. You hear all the silent court cases including Ithica's," said Chief Justice Lylieberman.

"I didn't know we had silent court cases?" complained Judge Phillip Nobetter.

"It's part of being a judge," said Chief Justice Lylieberman.

"And Jack here, Judge Jack Bastian, makes those judgements?" asked Phillip Nobetter.

"No, no... normally the person's already silenced in jail or an asylum. I just fill out the paperwork. It's usually my signature or my electronic signature. But I'm always told what I've signed if it's electronic," explained Jack.

"And the judiciary insists you do this?" questioned Judge Phillip Nobetter.

"I was chosen... They might be going rogue and know information or experienced things military intelligence want kept secret. It's normal."

"In Australia?" questioned Phillip Nobetter again.

"Yeah, in Australia, but Jack can do his paperwork anywhere. Sometimes he's in a detox centre," said Chief Justice Lylieberman while laughing.

"That is true," said Jack.

"But what does Ithica do?" asked Phillip Nobetter again.

"What we have to," said Defence Minister Barry Porfellow.

"Am I not allowed to know?" asked Phillip Nobetter.

"You know more now than a lot of the people who've worked there," said Barry Porfellow.

Phillip Nobetter looked confused.

"You're looking at this badly Phillip," said Barry Porfellow. "Like Defence ministers before me, it's part of my job."

"Is it really?" questioned Phillip Nobetter.

"Once, I had the terrible situation where intelligence was sending someone who was the son of a dear friend. They were sending him on a suicide mission. They knew he wouldn't be returning. They knew that.

I ripped into intelligence for that. I shouldn't have been put in that position. The guy should have been swapped out for someone else."

"That's so terrible," said Dugal.

"Yes, it was," added Barry Porfellow.

"So why close Ithica down and get rid of people?" asked Autumn.

"Too many secrets. Too many dead bodies," said Barry Porfellow. "Sometimes you have to reset."

"So why do we have to die too?" asked Dugal.

"Yes, do tell us Barry. Why the sudden rush to kill judges, and me?" asked Autumn.

"You're part of the problem. Not the solution," replied Barry. "I'm only telling you what Pete Jacobs told me."

"And you have no problem with that?" asked Autumn.

"It's not my doing. You know Defence and intelligence take orders from Pete Jacobs. I don't like the guy. I can't stand him. Some people shouldn't have been killed, particularly the judges," said Barry Porfellow.

"None of the judges should have been murdered," said Dugal.

"I agree," said Barry Porfellow. "And the people who escaped Ithica shouldn't have been taken back and killed. Like Anthea something who escaped to Carcoar. I forget her surname."

"Anthea was taken back to Ithica?" asked Autumn.

"She was forced, yes," said Barry Porfellow.

"And they killed her?" asked Autumn, now feeling a tear build in her left eye.

"Not yet," said Barry Porfellow.

"Good," said Autumn.

A couple of the judges nodded in agreement with Autumn. They didn't know Autumn and Anthea knew each other, or how.

Autumn had become pregnant to Georgio in her mid-twenties. She'd thought it impossible to have a child and run her business. Rather than abortion, she paid for Anthea's father to look after Anthea. This hadn't worked, though. Georgio was murdered and disappeared, leaving Anthea to be cared for.

Becoming adopted, Anthea's new parents moved overseas to somewhere in Europe, and Autumn soon lost contact with Anthea and them.

Fifteen years later, Autumn discovered the couple had divorced soon after arriving in Europe and sent Anthea back to an orphanage in Australia. Anthea then lived in more than seventeen care homes before escaping at sixteen.

Autumn had kept an eye on her daughter, not knowing what to do or say. She knew Anthea was tough.

"We have to stick together here," said Autumn now to the others around her. "We have to protect each other, like we've done in the past. Before Pete Jacobs became so powerful."

"So powerful," came Pete Jacobs' voice through the sound system. He was now visible on the large overhead screens.

All were quiet and fearful.

"Your days of freedom are over. All of you have gone unchallenged. Protecting each other and making secret pacts, wasting the superiority and independence you gained as judges. All of you... duplicitous with treachery for your own greed," said Pete Jacobs.

Chapter 11
Paper Clips

Closing the hall door to Pete Jacobs office Anthea was immediately shocked.

"Who are these people?" was her immediate reaction. Strangers. A slim, undernourished guy in his twenties was sitting in Kate's chair.

"Where's Kate?" asked Anthea.

"Who,? said the young guy, now spinning on his office chair.

"What happened?" asked Anthea.

"How did you get here?" the guy asked.

"Through that door."

"I saw that, but it doesn't open."

Anthea was careful with her answer.

"Do you have a name?" she asked.

"Of course I've got a name, but it's irrelevant... like yours."

A woman behind Anthea started crying uncontrollably.

The guy immediately made hand gestures indicating to others to take the woman away.

"What happened? Where's she going?" questioned Anthea.

"Three co-workers took their own lives in the bathroom. They're taking her to her pod. She can cry there and come back when she's finished," said the guy.

"I'm going to my Pod," Anthea said quietly to the guy.

"I have to stay here. I'm afraid to be alone," responded the guy.

This didn't make sense to Anthea. There were her and the guy left in the room.

Anthea moved quickly to her Pod, hoping to see no one. Once inside, she used duct tape and sealed the door.

She had failed to kill Jacobs and more people were dead.

Lying on her back, she felt the pain in her neck and shoulders.

She hadn't seen her former boss for several years. It was difficult to gauge how different he was.

Pete Jacobs had been across her every move, though. That didn't happen previously. Or did it? No. That did happen before. Jacobs kept it quiet.

"Anthea, we need to talk. Callam sent me. He needs to see you," said a voice in her pod.

Anthea ignored the voice at first. She didn't want to see Callam. Hearing it three times, she firmly replied.

"I'm not talking to Callam. He said the same yesterday. He's had plenty of chances to tell me what's so important. I turned up at Pythons, some twenty-three-year-old pole dancer said his name was Liam. Told me to follow him, went to an all-night diner and ended up sleeping with him. I thought I was drugged. Except when I woke up this morning, he was still there. Naturally I left."

"Look on your screen."

Anthea looked and saw a small pink pulsating dot.

"I'm Shay. Can I come on your screen?"

"After last night with Liam, I really don't care."

Shay appeared on Anthea's monitor.

"Holy hell," said Anthea, looking at the naked Shay on her screen.

"Callam is in trouble."

"Oh, do tell," said Anthea. "He works for intelligence. Did he forget? You're his mentor. Go do something."

"It's more complicated. You saw Pete Jacobs. What did you think...?"

"I think his anger-management lessons are starting to work. He told me to kill myself. Oh, and he's going to kill everyone at Ithica."

"Did he mention SET 24?" asked Shay.

"No. But Jacobs isn't the reminiscing type. He obliterates, kills, moves on."

"He's AI."

"No, he's not."

"Did you really see him?"

Anthea wondered how he was able to move around so quickly. Was he a hologram?

"He's not a hologram." said Shay.

"I didn't say he is." Anthea angrily replied.

"You were thinking it, though."

"I don't need you to tell me what I was... or wasn't thinking."

"He's similar technology to me. Screen only. You felt intoxicated or woozy when you arrived in his office. You couldn't see he was appearing on different screens. It all seemed hazy," said Shay.

Shay described it well, but she wasn't going to admit it.

"So who controls AI Pete Jacobs?" Anthea asked.

"Jacobs does. You didn't hear what happened when you were holidaying in Carcoar?" said Shay.

"I wasn't holidaying."

"I've seen the holiday pics... Peter Jacobs created an AI version to replace himself. Called him Pete Jacobs. Now you're up to date."

Anthea remained quiet.

"It gets worse," Shay added quickly. "Peter Jacobs had all the participants at SET 24 create mentors. The data was used to create his AI monster. Callam was supposed to be destroyed. Luckily he wasn't... otherwise I wouldn't be here."

"Pete Jacobs' AI is running Ithica?" questioned Anthea.

"Pete Jacobs is bad AI. Without conscience or humanity. A million times worse than his creator. His endgame is to destroy everyone who's superfluous."

Anthea remained quiet.

"Compared to AI, humans are expensive to run. Far less capable, no reliability. You have a very small productive period. There's nine months lost just carrying the creature around before birth and not all humans can do that. Then when the article is born it's still unproductive for years and must be taught."

"It's called a baby," said Anthea.

"And your obsessed with four letter words," added Shay.

"Are you a mentor or a menace?" asked Anthea.

"I'm not evil. I'm Callam's mentor. Unlike other mentors. I've still got my mentee."

"Your what?"

"Mentee, the person I'm mentoring."

"None of this makes sense."

"Pete Jacobs still needs something from you. Then he'll destroy you."

"Look, if you're being helpful, try harder," said Anthea.

"I'm not your mentor."

"Obviously."

Anthea thought about Pete Jacobs being AI. It frightened her. She sensed she might have a panic attack. Why did Pete Jacobs want her alive?

"Callam needs to see you at Pythons," said Shay.

"And what's the theme tonight? Show and tell?"

> "Oooh. That's cruel," said Shay, putting his leg up to hide his shlong.

"He's got you. Why does he need me?"

"You're a physical presence. I appear on screens and people only notice I'm naked and gorgeous. You don't have that problem."

"Careful, Shay. Are you going to tell me what Callam wants now?"

"He didn't tell me."

"Can you guess? You're his mentee. Is that seriously a word?"

"He wants to see you now."

"What, and leave people being killed here?" Anthea said, feeling frustrated. "Why can't he come here?"

"He said it's too dangerous here."

"So you asked him?"

"Yes. I have to protect him."

"I give up," said Anthea, stripping the black duct tape from her door.

"See you both at Pythons," said Anthea while tying her hair back and putting on a cap.

"Anthea, I'm here to help you too. Not just Callam. If I lose Callam I disappear like you. Pete Jacobs is far more powerful and cleverer than you and me combined. We have to remember that. And use it. That's all we've got. We have to outsmart him."

"Look, Shay, I know you're here to help. I have trust issues...and Ithica's a death sentence."

"Ithica's not the worst," said Shay. "The judiciary's worse. They enable this to happen."

Anthea nodded.

"You have to go," said Shay before vanishing.

Anthea took a deep sigh, then opened her Pod door quietly, carefully making her way to the lift without anyone seeing her. She'd appear on security screens. That was normal.

Once out of the building, Anthea headed up Sussex Street towards Pythons. Soon, the street was busy with people. Loud fire engines had gathered at the bottom of an apartment building on the far side of Bathurst Street. Looking up, Anthea could see smoke.

Finally something that wasn't hidden, she thought to herself.

Ithica always hid their fires. The exact information was always changed.

Anthea stood looking at the commotion. More ambulances were arriving, as were more police cars. A police van labelled riot squad arrived. Its police jumped onto the footpath, immediately blocking everyone, including fire and ambulance staff.

Anthea then saw firefighters come out of the building. It seemed the fire was out.

Walking up Bathurst Street towards Hyde Park, she wondered why Callam had to see her.

Crossing Elizabeth Street, she walked into Hyde Park Anthea looked at the monument ahead of her. The Anzac War Memorial.

Anthea remembered her conversation with a gay landscape designer. Some of the paths around the memorial formed the shape of a circumcised cock shooting into the memorial pond. They had both laughed.

Sitting on the steps at the base of the memorial, Anthea thought about those killed. Anthea couldn't help but remember some of the people. That was it. They were people. To Australian Defence and intelligence they were just items. Like paper clips.

Anthea looked at the Pool of Remembrance. To Anthea it was a pack of lies. So was *Lest We Forget*. It was all such a bloody mess.

It was too much. Anthea wiped tears from her face with her hands, but the tears kept coming. She tried to be quiet, but that was difficult too. She knew other people were walking by and seeing her distressed. Soon the tears became sobbing. It was uncontrollable.

Her life had been for nothing. A series of unhappy memories, getting worse as the years went on. She should have stayed in Carcoar. It would have been better to die slowly there from cold and hunger. Stupidly, she had always thought being an Australian was lucky. She'd been told it was.

Callam didn't need to see her. What was she going to say? Yes Callam, they're going to kill us. He was the reason she was back in Sydney.

She had stupidly thought in returning she could take revenge. But there were far too many involved. Far too much had been stolen. She thought she would try to save lives. Help people.

She looked up to see six, then eight, more police officers around her.

"You can't sit here," a young buxom female cop said to her.

Anthea was still crying while a sniffer dog climbed over her legs. Anthea prevented the dog from sniffing between her legs. The dog snarled at her.

"Do you live here?" said another young male cop.

"No, it's a park."

Anthea looked at the police officer. He wasn't wearing a badge.

"I need to see ID," said another cop, again not wearing a badge number.

"I haven't got any," replied Anthea.

"Your mobile then," said the first cop.

Anthea wiped her eyes, tried to stop crying as best she could, and handed over her phone.

"You need to open it," said the first cop, handing the mobile back.

"Do you realise it's an offence to sit on these steps?" said the second cop.

"What? No way," said Anthea, handing her mobile back.

"I think you're lying," said the second cop.

"What, why would I lie?"

"Tim, this phone has no contact list on it, nor recent phone calls. No records. I can't tell who she is. No apps. Could be a burner phone," said the first cop to the second.

The second cop looked sternly at Anthea before looking at a female officer standing close by.

"Stephanie, can you have a look at this? No ID on her, her phone doesn't tell us anything, and she's seriously breaking the law."

The female police officer looked at Anthea's phone before staring at Anthea.

"Lady, I'm going to ask this question only once. If you lie, or I don't like your answer, I'm going to charge you with obstruction of justice, hindering a police enquiry, and everything else. I know you're crying, but that's no excuse for breaking the law."

"What have I done?" said Anthea.

"I said name," Stephanie said angrily.

"Anthea Tonelli."

Stephanie and other police officers looked on their phones and talked amongst themselves. Anthea couldn't hear their conversations.

"This is a penalty notice for sitting on these steps. You should have read the sign, at the top of the steps, before sitting here," said the first cop.

"I didn't see the sign," explained Anthea.

"Just because you can't see a sign doesn't mean there isn't one," Stephanie said angrily.

Anthea stood up and took the folded notice. She remained quiet, waiting for the police and dog to go.

Opening the penalty, the fine was $2,200.

"Lest we fuckin forget," said Anthea watching the eight officers proceed towards a homeless man lying passed out on a park bench.

Feeling afraid, Anthea knew better than to stay and see what the police did next. The man would be threatened and possibly taken away. If the homeless man had fought for his country, he'd spent the rest of his life wondering why.

Anthea headed towards Pythons to see what was so urgent.

She could see scaffolding and construction workers at Pythons erecting a hoarding for the entire building.

Getting closer, the men were all wearing new clothes, new white shoes. It was more like a fashion runway shoot for a gay spread. Topless hunks showing off their chiselled bodies. Some concentrating on their reflections in the windows. Anthea smelt intelligence.

She knew the scent too well. The kind of smell where nothing makes sense, and the supposed disguise stands out like an infectious boil on the person's forehead.

The front door of Pythons was open. There was a surveillance vehicle across the road. Anthea was used to overkill. The bigger question was: why Pythons?

She climbed through the scaffolding to get to the front door. Inside, the place had been raided. Mirrors were smashed. Light fittings down. Wires stripped, and a smell of something she'd never smelt before. Anthea assumed it was all right to breathe as undercover tradespeople were walking through.

Further in, the building looked more like a bomb site. Rubble everywhere. Looking at what was the bar area, Anthea recognised the barman she'd spoken to.

Anthea slowly approached the guy.

"Can I get you anything?" asked Anthea.

"My life back. No, I want a different one."

"What happened?"

"You tell me. Your guys ram-raided us from the rear last night. They were really quiet. About five am. Blacked out the security cameras. Opened the rear doors. Took people away, including upstairs. Told rich fuckers upstairs to disappear, say nothing, or they'll be dead too."

"Is that what they said? They'll be dead too?" Anthea carefully asked.

"Yeah."

Looking around, Anthea wondered why Pythons had been targeted.

"You trying to work it out too?" said the bartender.

Anthea nodded. "It doesn't make sense."

"You know it's a war now," said the barman.

"War?" asked Anthea.

"Yeah."

"With who?" asked Anthea. "Who are you?"

"With Jacobs, with Ithica."

"Why do you think it's Pete Jacobs?" asked Anthea.

"You can smell it yourself. You can. You know what your agency smells like. You smelt it when you walked in here."

"But why? Pete Jacobs?"

"Honey, I know you're smarter than you look. You were forced to work for the wrong side."

"But—" Anthea said, trying to interrupt.

"Butts around here are cheap. You saw that last night. I told you.We have better intelligence. You just learnt Pete Jacobs is AI. That's slow. Returning from Carcoar, you really aren't up to speed. We knew Peter Jacobs was creating Pete. We watched it happening."

"I just thought Pythons was a well organised gay bar."

"Was... So why are you here?"

Anthea remained quiet.

"You saw what's happening outside. You raided the place and closed it down. But you still came in. What did Shay tell you?"

"Shay...?"

"Callam's screen fuck buddy... I wish he was real."

"Callam. Shay told me to come here... but you probably know that."

"True," said the bartender. "And you're asking where's Callam?"

"Yes."

"Not about Liam and Gier?"

"Yes, of course, but—" said Anthea.

"Forget the butts. Callam was taken away. I don't know where. Truly. Liam didn't work here last night. He was abducted by three of your judges before he arrived. Three judges with grudges."

Anthea was quiet.

"Gier's here. Upstairs. Came back about an hour ago."

"Is there anything else?" asked Anthea.

"Pete Jacobs' AI is biased. He bases his decisions on his prejudices. He has an ego, and kindness to him is weakness. His decisions will always be prejudiced. Remember that. I'm interested to see who kills him first."

"But I don't know who you work for," said Anthea.

"And you don't need to. So much for Australian intelligence. You've all been too busy stealing everything you can," said the barman.

"They've destroyed Pythons," she said.

"They destroyed Pythons. Not us."

"People keep disappearing," said Anthea.

"And it worries you?"

"Yes."

"Well, with AI in control, it's going to get a lot worse. You know that."

Anthea nodded in agreement.

"I'm tired of seeing people disappear. Everything's kept quiet."

"I know," said the barman.

"I didn't ask your name," said Anthea.

"You did. I didn't tell you. I'm the barman... People's names aren't important anymore..."

Anthea stared at the man.

"I could join your agency."

The barman coughed and spluttered, taken aback by Anthea's words.

"Darling, you're the most damaged person I've ever met. Some people live through a couple of war zones before escaping. You don't escape. You keep rushing back. You came up on our radar when you were born. You're second-generation intelligence. Your father disappeared while playing with you in a park."

"That's my earliest memory, being left on the swing."

"You learnt first-hand what adoption and care homes are like. Children disappearing. You're obsessed with disappearances. You can't look at a group of people without wondering, probing how many people in the group have disappeared or been killed. There's crime and murder in everything you see."

"But it's true," said Anthea.

"For you it is... You see crime everywhere. No country can deal with the amount of crime you're uncovering. It's part of your DNA... but nobody wants to know... Your concept of law is outdated."

"Will your agency kill me?"

"No need. You'll do that yourself."

"It makes me angry, so many people want me dead."

"Understandably, they're defending themselves. Knowledge isn't power... It's a Pandora's box."

Chapter 12
Grease and oil change

Climbing through more glass and debris, Anthea cut her hand on a piece of broken mirror.

"Fuck," she said, wrapping it with cloth. She saw reflections of herself in the cracked pieces of mirror.

"Totally broken. I look totally broken."

Her world had changed. Again. Some total stranger claiming to be a barman knew everything about her. He'd summed her up in seconds.

She'd taken the slow road accumulating forty-eight years of catastrophe, or thirty-eight years when she was speaking to Liam, and for what? What was the end? Live... She remembered Shay saying humans are obsessed with four-letter words. Life. Fuck. Hate. She'd taken the wrong road. It was all so exhausting. She sat knowing she had a collection of bad thoughts.

Anthea now saw her ideas, judgements were all wrong. Life wasn't her choice. It happened. She always found something to escape from. The barman was right.

She hadn't realised there was a different side though. She hadn't seen it. She didn't have access. She was spending all her time genuinely trying to help people. Except for the people she'd killed.

What the barman said was correct. She would kill herself helping people.

Was it really such a simple question? Was there an alternative to Ithica? No. Like so many others, Ithica would say she disappeared; in truth her body would be dumped somewhere.

Anthea had never found the dumping ground for the many hundreds of bodies. There was an inventory including a list of recruits who died during their torture.

For the first time, Anthea saw she was a slave to her masters at Ithica.

Her thoughts were interrupted by a noise from her mobile. She'd turned her mobile to silent.

Looking, she felt more exasperated seeing a dot on her screen. It was Shay. He'd sent her to Pythons to see Callam. Urgent, he'd said. Anthea was surprised Callam was still alive despite having Shay for a mentor. She would ignore Shay.

"Can we talk?" Shay whispered to Anthea.

"I'm ignoring your call," said Anthea.

"It's important. Where's Callam?"

"I don't know. You're his mentor."

"I don't know where he is all the time."

"Obviously. Otherwise you wouldn't keep harassing me. And why don't you know where he is?"

"He doesn't want me too."

"Ridiculous. You're his mentor."

Both Shay and Anthea stared at each other. Anthea was waiting for Shay to answer. Shay was supposed to be monitoring and helping Callam full time. It wasn't up to Callam to say when.

"Callam wants his own space. He only wants to see me sometimes. I'm supposed to be his mentor, but he created me to be one of his fuck buddies."

"I can see that," said Anthea, once again looking at Shay's overly large appendage. "Why is your cock always appearing just below the middle of the screen?"

"Callam asked SET 24 if he could have two mentors. They told him no."

"Good. Ithica should have operated out of Pythons," said Anthea.

"And Callam doesn't listen to me. I can give him ten reasons why he shouldn't do something and he'll still do it. Getting you from Carcoar. I told him no."

"What?" said Anthea. "You advised him not to collect me from Carcoar?"

"Yes, of course I did," said Shay. "When Callam brought you back his usefulness was over. I can only think he's alive because I'm still here. When they kill him, I'm gone too. That's what happens to mentors."

"You told Callam not to collect me?"

"Yes, if Callam didn't bring you here you'd still be in Carcoar dying slowly ."

Anthea hesitated before replying. It was true.

"So many people are disappearing, Shay. It's the end of Ithica."

"Did you hear what I said, Anthea? I'm gone when Callam's gone."

"You're right. And I'm gone too," said Anthea.

Anthea and Shay stared at each other.

"I found human beings often think about death, or think they're about to die when they don't. If you died every time you thought you're about to die.. there'd be no humans left."

"I'm only thinking about it," said Anthea.

"What is there to think about?" asked Shay.

"My existence will be suppressed," said Anthea.

"Looking at your life so far. Does it matter?" asked Shay.

"Aren't you a mentor?" said Anthea. "Or Callam's mentor?"

Anthea watched Shay roll his eyes.

"I'm tired of seeing Australians secretly killed," said Anthea. "So many people know it's happening but do nothing. Australian media, judges... everyone remains silent."

"You'll find Gier upstairs," said Shay. "I'll get back to you."

Anthea was surprised when Shay disappeared.

Reaching the lift, Anthea saw it was severely damaged. Luckily a passageway next to the lift showed a flight of stairs.

She would look for Geir. Wandering carefully through the first floor she was careful not to make noise. Some of the attackers might still be in the building. She knew better than to call out. Clothes, possessions, sex toys and drinks were strewn everywhere. People had left hastily.

Venturing onto the second floor, Anthea found Gier stretched out on a chaise in a cloud of marijuana smoke.

"Hi killer girl. There's plenty of coke in the champagne bucket. Over there... a tray of colours," said Gier, pointing in the wrong direction.

"And there's something I have to tell you," said Gier. "I got a pile of hash here too," said Gier, pointing to the hash with his cigarette.

Anthea watched as a few embers fell onto the hash and lit.

A small fire formed. Anthea slowly walked towards the fire, bent down and casually put it out. Gier looked at Anthea but seemingly didn't comprehend the pile was alight.

"The barman downstairs said I'd find you here."

"Jack Daniels," said Gier. "Good guy. Is he still down there? Amazing."

Anthea could see Gier was high. She didn't know what else he'd taken besides marijuana. Hopefully nothing. It was useless to ask.

"What do you have to tell me?" asked Anthea.

"Everyone's gone... everyone... wow... I didn't see this coming," Gier said, raising his hand in the air. It was like air punching.

"They killed him. Callam's dead. I saw them kill him." Added Gier.

"No," said Anthea. "The barman downstairs said they took Callam away during the raid."

"Was he dead or alive?" asked Gier.

"I assumed alive, and I just saw Shay."

"Who?" asked Gier.

"Sorry, one of Callam's fuck buddies."

"Does he come to Pythons?"

"Not really... But you said earlier you saw people, someone kill Callam."

"Did I? Was that what I had to tell you? It wasn't Callam. It couldn't have been Callam. Why do you think Callam's dead?" said Gier.

Anthea now saw Gier was more out of it than she thought and had possibly taken cocaine and other stimulants.

"Why did you come back to Pythons?" asked Anthea.

"To see Callam. We want him to move to Studs," said Gier.

"It's not that simple. He can't just leave," responded Anthea.

"That's what Callam says."

"It's all a giant mess. The barman downstairs said three judges with grudges abducted Liam. Do you know where they took Liam?" asked Anthea.

"Liam's gone too? We have to save him. They'll kill him."

"The judges will kill him?" asked Anthea.

"No, the kidnappers will. You should have told me. The kidnappers will kill Liam when the judges don't pay them. Like before."

"Before?" questioned Anthea.

"The judges have done it before. They won't pay the kidnappers. Give them stay-out-of-jail cards instead. The kidnappers then kill the guys they captured. Judges get away with it. It usually ends badly. No. It always ends badly," said Gier.

"What three judges?" she asked.

"Bastian, Leech, and Morus," said Gier.

Anthea was familiar with all three.

"They always hang out together at Pythons," said Gier.

Anthea remembered the three went through Sydney University together. Graduated together. All three became barristers, then judges soon after.

"I could never work out how they became judges so soon after becoming barristers until I saw they all work for intelligence," said Anthea.

Gier was hesitant to say anything.

"But why kidnap Liam?" asked Anthea.

"That's what they do," replied Gier.

"But they're judges. What do you mean, that's what they do? And who are these kidnappers?" asked Anthea.

"Just criminals."

"So why not pay them?" said Anthea.

"Have you ever tried to get money out of a judge?"

Anthea nodded in agreement.

"We have to rescue Liam," said Gier. "They'll kill him. It's their stay-out-of-jail card. They'll never set foot in another courtroom again after they kill Liam."

"But why did the judges kidnap Liam anyway? Do I want to know?" asked Anthea.

"Jealousy."

"Jealous? That's ridiculous."

"They're jealous for different reasons. Yes, they're all grandiose narcissists. Judge Leech feels inadequate because he's only a family court judge... and he's worried Liam is being unfaithful," said Gier.

"Unfaithful? He's a male prostitute in a gay bar. And he's straight."

"I think bisexual might be closer."

"Last night I was convinced Liam's completely hetero," said Anthea.

"Well at Pythons he's top shelf gay... Them judges are trying to control everyone. Especially Bastian... His judicial days are over. He used to be a military judge. Did a lot of dirty work for military. No conscience. Then they put him in charge of signing off silent cases. They don't need Bastian to sign off though. By the time Bastian gets the case they're in jail, a mental asylum, or dead. They don't need his autograph. Bastian sees that," said Gier.

"So Bastian sees he's dead?" said Anthea.

"I wish they'd get rid of my father," said Gier.

"You said the judges with grudges have killed before."

"Yes, and it went horribly wrong... You work for intelligence. How come you don't know this?"

Anthea remained quiet while Gier continued.

"Last one would have been Luca. From North Queensland. He was adorable."

"What happened?" asked Anthea. Now realising there was so much she didn't know.

"He'd just had his nineteenth birthday and was going to uni. They took a liking to him. He became another missing person."

"But why allow the judges back into Pythons?"

"And raise questions?" said Gier.

Anthea sat looking at Gier. It had been a mistake to return. Anthea reached out to Gier and tried to wake him.

"Gier, Gier, can you get yourself out of here? Go back to Tim and Jason at the farm? And be careful."

"What? Yes," said Gier, waking.

"Are you sure?" asked Anthea.

"But I can help."

"No, it's better if you go back to Tim and Jason. Go to Studs. Callam might escape and go there. I have to find Liam. Shay will help me."

"So you want me to go back to the farm?"

"Yes... now."

Anthea quickly stood up and left Gier lying on the chaise. Going downstairs, she pulled out her mobile.

She tried to find Liam's location. Timelines displayed movements of his sightings.

A street surveillance camera showed Liam walking towards Pythons. Then two people wearing black clothes and balaclavas jumping out of a black van and abducting him.

Tracing the movements of the three judges was much easier. All three carried their mobiles and their movements were simple to follow.

The three judges were separately heading towards the original abandoned Ithica building. There was no indication of Liam though.

Shay now appeared on Anthea's mobile.

"I've found the three judges," Shay proudly announced.

"Terrific," said Anthea.

"They're on Justice Bastian's yacht moored at the Cruising Yacht Club in Rushcutters Bay."

"No, they aren't," said Anthea, wondering why or how Shay got it wrong.

Checking, Anthea responded, "They were there yesterday. And where's Liam? You've got the wrong day, Shay."

"What?"

"I've got the judges and the van at the abandoned Ithica building," Anthea said, checking the three judges' whereabouts again. "The black van's there. I can't find Liam, though."

"That's good," said Shay.

Anthea was again surprised by Shay's response. He wasn't making sense. Shay was preoccupied with something. It wasn't like him to get things wrong. Something was amiss.

"No, I said I can't find Liam."

"He'll be somewhere," said Shay.

"Shay, did you really just say somewhere... like... somewhere... what's happening? Liam has been abducted by three judges with grudges who have murdered people before. They're about to kill him."

"I can't find Callam."

"Well, I'm sure he's somewhere... I mean," Anthea quickly added, seeing her response was the same as Shay's.

"You said it," Shay quickly added.

"You know what I mean."

"Do I...? You're more interested in saving the guy who gave you a long overdue grease and oil change."

Anthea gasped. She tried to conceal it. What had just happened? Where had Shay's dialogue come from? His response. Had Shay heard it from someone? If so, why was he repeating it?

Anthea thought better than to show surprise, but she was totally shocked. Shay was an AI app. How had it happened? Perhaps he'd been compromised. Pete Jacobs. Anthea only knew she couldn't trust Shay as much as she had. She should have thought about her reliance on Shay sooner.

Was she making too much of it? Should she have just replied saying something like, yeah, well, Liam's grease will keep me going? It's more than you get from Callam. She was now glad she didn't.

Was there a right way to deal with this? She would have to wait and see. She needed Shay to help her rescue Liam, if she could. Shay was more concentrated on saving Callam.

"I'm not getting Callam's vital signs. I think he's dead," said Shay. "Even when I don't know where he is, I still get his body temperature, pulse rate, etc. I can tell when he's having sex."

"Good for you," said Anthea.

"I need to save him, Anthea. If I don't, I'm gone too."

Anthea knew Shay was correct. Maybe he wasn't, though. Shay was operating in larger computer networks than originally intended. Shay was designed to be a low-energy-use, screen-and-audio-only, helpful AI unit, unlike what Pete Jacobs had become.

As such, and as Shay said himself, he would help Anthea.

"Shay, I need us to save Liam first. And I need your help to save him. You may disagree, but I need to override you. Callam has survival skills. Liam has none. Also, I'm one of the human beings you're supposed to help first."

"Liam doesn't work for intelligence. I'm supposed to assist intelligence agents first," said Shay.

"That would be me."

"Liam might already be dead," said Shay.

"If that was true, why would the judges meet the men in the van? It's only to get Liam. He has to be alive."

Anthea tried to convince herself Liam was still living.

She knew she was failing. She'd been stupid to think she could achieve anything. Callam telling her she could use her silent-kill skills to save people. She just had to kill people to save people. Callam had really convinced her.

And she'd done it.

Chapter 13
Advance Australia Fair

"Was Liam still alive?" She'd asked the same question many times before. The answer was usually no. Was Callam still alive? That was probably no, too.

She'd made her way to a secret entrance at the old Ithica base Shay said was best.

"Mobile, mobile... mobile," she said, searching through her bag. It wasn't there. "No," she said, remembering she'd placed it in her dress pocket.

"You're thinking again," Shay said quietly.

Anthea didn't answer.

"Have they definitely got Liam inside?" asked Anthea.

"Yes."

"Definitely?" asked Anthea. "And this is the correct way there?"

"We've been over this Anthea. Yes, the Navy base has grown a lot since you escaped to Carcoar. The plans I showed you are correct. It's Commonwealth land. They've reclaimed a lot of land from Sydney Harbour for additional warships. They've built a missile silo, so four of the access tunnels to Ithica are gone. This is the best access tunnel to use, with entry to a rabbit warren of tunnels at various points should you need to hide."

"Are you sure it's a missile silo?"

"Are we saving Liam or discussing disadvantages of locating missile silos in built-up residential areas?" said Shay.

"Saving Liam."

"You were hesitant."

"No... no. I need to know Liam's still alive."

"He is currently, but if you keep hesitating he won't be."

"I need everything to go well, Shay."

"This is a first. Since when?"

"Now!" exclaimed Anthea.

"Why the change...? I was just getting used to your catastrophes."

"You think I chose this job? For me it was this or death. Human beings can be very cruel."

"I'd drop the word human if I was you," said Shay.

Anthea stood up and readied herself. She had memorised the passageways and revised layout of Ithica. Liam was in the second-lowest level. Shay guided her.

Once inside the tunnel, Anthea made her way to the first of many secret passageways. She noticed Ithica was still occupied. Corridors cut out of stone were still dimly lit.

"Wrong way," said Shay.

Anthea was surprised.

"But we could go this way."

"If we wanted to go out and back in again," said Shay. "We're nearly there."

It seemed true. Getting closer, Anthea occasionally heard muffled sounds. Presumably from Liam and his captors. Sometimes yells. Other times moaning. She thought the worst and moved hesitantly closer.

Plans showed the area Laim was in was caged with bars. There were four separate isolation cells at the back of the cage.

Still listening to moaning, Anthea climbed up on some rocks and peered down. She was horrified. Liam was being impaled by Justice Leech while sucking Justice Bastian's long, thick cock.

"He's saving himself," said Shay. "And doing a fine job."

Anthea remained silent, watching Liam saving himself. He was on all fours, then flipped on his back by a young guy before licking Leech's arse. Justice Morus joined them, along with another two young guys in their twenties. Anthea didn't recognise the young guys. Perhaps they had captured Liam in their van. All six men were intertwined and showed no sign of giving up.

"It's his job," said Shay.

"He does it too well. Either the judges finish first or we're going to be here for a very long time. Who are the two young guys anyway? Are they the captors? Liam would have jumped in their van gladly."

"No. The judges hired them. They work for an agency like Liam."

"They're not his captors then?" questioned Anthea.

"No, they're upstairs."

Both Anthea and Shay continued looking as the six guys continually fucked each other. Justice Bastian attempted to take a rest on a nearby sofa, but one of the guys and Liam dragged him back to the main podium. There was no sign of the action ending.

"What's it feel like seeing your boyfriend having sex with other guys? I'd like to know," said Shay. "I know when Callam's having sex even if I can't see it. I wish AI could do feelings."

"I'm probably the wrong person to ask, Shay. I block my emotions. To survive. Being AI without emotions, you're probably more suited to working at Ithica. And I'm seeing Liam is more bisexual than he lets on."

"He's very convincing as a gay."

"He tells me he's straight."

"I know, and you've found it's hard... it's very hard," said Shay, looking again at the men.

"He's very persuasive."

Shay remained looking at the group.

"I wish one of the guys was Callam," said Shay.

"It's hugely sexy looking at a group of guys playing. Football doesn't come close. Liam looks to be controlling the action. Making sure everyone's enjoying themselves, getting their fair share of play," said Anthea.

"He's like a ringmaster."

"We're supposed to be rescuing Liam," said Anthea.

"Do you think he'll want to leave?... I mean," added Shay.

"I don't know, Shay," said Anthea, sighing. "He really fooled me, and Callam introduced us. Here we are worried about them. They don't worry about us. Nothing."

"It's my job," said Shay.

"It's not mine. They should have sent you to Carcoar, Shay. You would have told me to stay there."

Anthea noticed Justice Leech walk away from the group to take a piss. On his return he inspected the bars and gates, finding everything locked. He whispered to Bastian, who told Morus. Soon all three judges were walking around the cage looking for an opening. Liam noticed as well: they were all locked in.

"OK... get us out of here," Jack Bastian yelled through the locked iron gate.

Neander Leech asked, "What are they doing, Jack?"

"I said get us out of here," Jack yelled again. "The idiots are having fun," Jack replied, looking at Leech.

"Time's up... enough with the games... get us out," Morus yelled, trying to be louder than Bastian.

"Good one, Morus... I don't see them coming though," said Jack.

"Perhaps they're doing something," replied Morus.

"The excuses you give. Listen to yourself sometimes... or read your own judgements," replied Jack.

"You know my tipstaff writes my judgements," Morus said quietly.

"Gentlemen," interrupted Neander Leech, seeing one of Liam's captors now standing on the other side of the bars.

"Gentlemen," said the guy, aiming his gun at the judges.

"Scotty," responded Jack Bastian. "How's your brother?"

"You know I killed him. What's with the jokes?" said Scotty, raising his pistol and aiming it at Jack Bastian.

"Just trying to make light conversation."

"Yeah, well I'd go back to fucking if I was you...."

"Just trying to—" said Jack.

"Are you going to ask about my uncle, if you are... I'll kill you now."

"Not at all," said Neander, trying to protect Jack. "Where are the others?"

"What others?"

"The two guys who helped you in the van... captured Liam."

"Ned's studying to become AI, and Bowen is about to rescue a woman who's really stupid... isn't that right, Bowen?"

"It is, Scotty," a voice could be heard yelling. Anthea turned around to see a man with a gun.

Anthea was surprised. How had that happened? Shay should have seen him coming rather than watching the guys in front of him... coming.

Bowen moved his gun in the direction he wanted Anthea to go.

Walking towards the cage entrance, Anthea was then directed to join Liam in the closest of the four separate locked cells. The cell was the size of an SUV. The only items were a single bed against the end wall and a metal bucket next to the bed. Anthea and Liam sat on opposite ends of the bed looking at each other. Bowen locked them in.

"You shouldn't have come," Liam whispered to Anthea.

Anthea rummaged in her pocket, produced a breath freshener, and threw it to him.

"Use it. It's not your breath, it's the BO and smell of cum on you."

Liam commenced doing as he was told, spraying under each arm pit, then rubbing it in before twisting his muscular body and developed arms searching for cum. He could see Anthea was looking.

"I think there's some back here," he said, rubbing his firm buttocks, before stroking his thickened cock for good luck. He moved a little closer to Anthea and held out his hand for her to take the breath freshener.

Both remained quiet, listening to the people outside. The three judges were now facing Scotty and Bowen. The two young guys had sat down on the podium as directed.

"Scotty, enough with the games. You forget we're judges," said Jack Bastian.

"I had a deal with you faggots. You wanted that guy captured. Am I right?"

"Yes," said Jack Bastian and Neander Leech. Moran Morus shook his head to indicate no.

"Hang on, he's saying no."

"He means yes," said Jack.

"Jack, Jack... Jack... I hate it when people argue with me like you are now... especially when I've got a gun."

All now looked at Moran Morus.

"I'm reconsidering... re-looking at the particular incident, I would now strongly argue the circumstances don't form the basis of a grudge. There aren't really the conditions here to substantiate—"

"Thank God you don't write your own judgements," Jack Bastian said loudly, interrupting Moran Morus.

"I'm looking at statute law, Jack."

"Well now look at their gun... and shut up," said Neander Leech.

"Right you are," said Scotty.

All three judges were now quiet. Jack Bastian was left to do the talking.

"Why the guns, Scotty. We have an agreement to pay you for abducting Liam."

"Ay, that you did, but you might want to sit down with your two grandsons over there."

"They're not our grandsons."

"Glad to hear it... I said sit."

The three judges joined the two young guys on the podium. The boys were now worried, like the three judges. All sat together, huddling and holding each other.

"I've had a better offer," said Scotty.

"For what?" asked Jack Bastian.

"For young Liam, the guy you were into ten minutes ago," said Scotty.

"I don't believe you," Jack Bastian quickly replied.

"Badly judged, Jack... "

"You just want more money."

"No, Jack... well actually yes... but I know your form. I didn't expect you or your mates to cough up. And as for promising to keep us out of jail... we're doing that ourselves...... Ned, who you haven't met... apart from becoming AI... is in his final year of studying film... He's hoping filming your get-together just now will launch him into the film industry. More likely the porn industry."

Jack looked at the other two judges and smiled.

"Scotty... judges are used to being extorted. This is nothing new. Everyone protects us. They need to. Australians need faith in their legal system. They need to know they can trust judges. When all else fails, people save us. And we get rid of vermin like you."

Anthea sat watching what was happening. Liam by now was sitting next to her to get a better view. Jack had stood to face Scotty. He was naked and looked around at the other men before staring back.

"So let us go and we'll forget this ever happened. I know I will... You're clearly making the wrong decisions here."

"It's not that simple, Jack," said Scotty. "You're not listening... I don't know who... but someone has bought you three judges."

"You can't buy us."

Scotty and Bowen laughed.

"Well someone has... and to be fair, I'll give you three the opportunity of buying your lives back. But there are rules... No appeals... no second chances... Each of you has to come up with the amount you'll pay me to live."

"That's ridiculous," said Neander.

"Isn't it just," said Scotty. "But it gets easier... Bowen has compiled a list of all your assets. Hidden overseas accounts. Bogus names... I just need to know how much you want to give me..."

"That's crazy," said Jack.

"It's fair, Jack. Australia is built on fairness. Isn't that crazy... Advance Australia Fair? Australia's national anthem. I don't know the lyrics. Do You?"

"I don't know either," said Jack.

"That doesn't surprise me Jack."

The two men stared at each other. For some reason the other judges had their heads down.

"I'm not rushing you on this Jack... and I'm going to release your grandsons so you can concentrate," said Scotty.

The two young guys were surprised. Another young guy appeared from upstairs.

"Ned's going to make sure you get out of here safely and you're not harassed by the military," said Scotty to the two young guys.

The two guys got up from the podium and hurried towards Scotty, nodding repeatedly and saying thank you. Bowen quickly relocked the gate.

The sexier guy asked Jack, "Thank you, Thank you... Can I give you a blow job or anything?"

Scotty smiled.

"I'll come with you. These judges have decisions to make," said Scotty.

Anthea and Liam looked at each other. The judges studied the pages they'd been given.

"They've listed everything," said Neander Leech.

"How did they find all this?" said Jack Bastian.

Liam and Anthea had been sitting together watching what was happening. Anthea waited for Liam to speak first. It became obvious.

"I can explain," said Liam to Anthea.

"No you can't, Liam, and there's no need," said Anthea.

"Do you think anyone will rescue us?" asked Liam.

"We're in the same boat as the judges," said Anthea.

"I was being real the other night," Liam said cautiously. "I like you."

Anthea remained quiet.

"How long were you watching me?" asked Liam.

"Long enough... to get aroused..."

"Some of them are hunks."

"I was talking about you," said Anthea.

"We have to get out of here," said Anthea.

"You say it as though it's easy."

Anthea smiled. She had no escape plan.

"Thanks for trying to rescue me Anthea. You're the only one," said Liam.

"Pythons is closed. There was a raid. No one was injured. Everyone got out," said Anthea.

The two looked through the bars. Each judge was reading silently, fearful.

Moran Morus had put his shirt, tie, and suit coat back on. He was naked from the waist down, having earlier soiled his trousers and thrown them aside. Neander Leech wore a singlet. Only Jack Bastian remained naked, writing furiously.

Hours passed. Anthea and Liam cuddled together. Liam put his arms around her. The judges left them alone, possessed by their own problems.

Scotty returned with Ned and Bowen, all carrying guns.

"OK... who's first?" asked Scotty.

The three judges were silent.

"Guys, mates... And I do think of you as mates.. Just not good mates. I know you take a long time with your judgements... We haven't got time. I need to know what figure you place on staying alive. You do the same in court every day."

Scotty sighed.

"OK, Neander Leech. From what I've seen of you playing with your grandsons, you've got the shortest straw. You can go first," said Scotty.

"What straws? I'm not doing this," said Neander.

"Seriously. You're not prepared to give up anything to remain alive?"

"I don't have to. People look after us. We're judges."

"No money at all? You wouldn't give anything to save yourself?"

"This is extortion. I'm not listening."

"Bad choice... really bad, really messy choice," said Scotty.

Scotty looked at Jack then turned to look at Bowen who smiled and nodded.

"Moran, you're next," said Scotty now spinning around and facing his target.

"I didn't get a straw," said Moran, confused.

"And God help anyone before you in a courtroom... You've been given pages showing your net worth. You agree?"

"It shows everything."

"Good. I'm glad to hear that... I hope you're not going to be stupid like Leech here. Given the chance to live, he says no... Says he'll be saved because he's a judge."

"You can't do this," said Moran.

"No... listen carefully. You're not listening. I'm asking you how much of your total worth you'll give me so you live? It can be a figure. It can be a percentage. Like one hundred percent.

"You can't do this," Moran repeated.

"Look if you can't hear me...ask Jack what I'm saying. Jack... can you get Moran to take this seriously.

Moran remained silent.

"Moran... You need to say a figure or a percentage. We all do," said Jack looking at Moran. Leech was still refusing to look at anyone.

"What will it be Moran? Do you think you should continue to live? So you can continue to destroy people every day with your prejudiced judgements?"

Scotty paused.

"Are any of you capable of making judgments for yourselves?" asked Scotty. "I'm not seeing it."

Scotty looked back towards Jack.

"This is very disappointing Jack. I expected more enthusiasm."

"We've been caught by surprise," replied Jack.

"You're all looking at this the wrong way. I'm trying to save your lives here," said Scotty.

"I appreciate everything you're doing... Scotty."

"I think the three of you should go and sit on the rock over there. I hate killing people. I really do."

"I know you do," said Jack.

Anthea and Liam watched the three judges return to the rock platform.

"You're next," said Scotty looking at Anthea and Liam. "Bowen get Liam and what's her name out."

Soon Anthea and Liam were standing outside the cage in front of Scotty.

"You can go," said Scotty.

Anthea shook her head. "Keep facing them," she told Liam. "It's a trick."

"It's not a trick, you idiot," said Scotty. "We were paid to capture Liam. The judges didn't pay us."

"I don't... it's not how this works," said Anthea.

"OK, have it your way," said Scotty.

Chapter 14

Like Death Row

Liam stripped down to his underpants and changed into a white T-shirt hanging on a doorknob.

"Wine," he said, taking a bottle and two large glasses from the refrigerator.

Anthea could see he was anxious, tense, and unable to concentrate, made obvious when he filled the two large glasses to the brim, draining the bottle.

She looked at how sexy he was. His biceps and pecs obvious in his shirt. Nipples protruding out.

"We can stay here in the dark and see anyone approaching," said Liam, sitting in an oversized sofa chair.

"For the rest of our lives," replied Anthea.

He gulped down his wine as if it were water.

"Do you think they'll come for us?" he asked.

"Of course. You know they will. Otherwise you wouldn't be hiding."

"But who?" asked Liam.

"There are too many who's..."

"The judges want me dead," said Liam.

"Not anymore. They have their own problems," said Anthea.

"And the police. Always wanted me dead," continued Liam.

"That isn't true... Pythons is full of gay cops. How can you say that?"

"Cops murdered my father... He had a law firm and took in a new partner. The partner and a couple of police used to bring drugs into the country. The cops were tipped off by Australian Customs. They set my father up to take the fall. The day before the court hearing my father was found hung in his garage. The drug case disappeared."

Anthea listened, but she'd heard it all before from so many people. "Dreadful."

"Then they tried to take my father's estate. Everything."

Anthea nodded.

"My mother died a year later before the estate was settled. She was run down by a car. Cops said she was in the wrong place at the wrong time. No police reports, no cameras, no mention by the media... it got worse after that."

Anthea remained quiet, feeling Liam's life was full of loose ends.

"I'm an only child... when my mother died I moved to Sydney and got the job at Pythons. I met Nigel Smatliefer there. He was a justice in the Supreme Court. He helped me a lot. I heard he died at his country property. Gier and I used to go there. I told him about my estate problems. He said he'd have a word to a few people... and it was taken care of."

Anthea was glad Liam knew Nigel was dead. Some things were too difficult. Like telling Liam she'd killed Justice Nigel Smatliefer practising silent kill.

"I was lucky. Nigel told me he couldn't help Gier though. Gier's father being Justice Mitchell Goot. He hates everyone, carries out vendettas, including against his own family and other judges," said Liam.

"It's truly a cruel world," said Anthea.

"My parents were good people, no criminal records. They knew I'm bisexual."

"Did they?" asked Anthea, seizing the chance to change the subject and discuss Liam's sexuality.

Liam awkwardly said, "Yes. Dad used to tell me about other bisexuals he knew or met. He tried to normalise my sexuality in his mind. Acceptance rather than tolerance. It was a start. Sometimes it was too difficult for him, though, when he heard things from his divorce cases."

"I'm fortunate you want to have sex with me," said Anthea, immediately smiling.

"Well, I understand it's not straightforward for you.

Anthea smiled before once again changing subjects. "We have to think about... the future."

"Are we discussing children or dogs?"

"Liam, it's serious... You were just abducted... You know what I'm talking about... People disappearing... Your parents."

"But it worked out."

"Your parents were murdered. How is that working out?" asked Anthea.

"I mean... You're right... I don't know... I'm still here. No one's killed me., said Liam.

Anthea could see Liam didn't know what to think. He was like her. Knowing people wanted you dead—but when?

"Knowing people want you dead... It's a continual thought, not even a thought. It's just there... but it isn't," said Liam.

"And it never goes away," said Anthea.

"No, it can't now. People will want to kill me for the rest of my life... I don't know who..."

"And nobody cares..." said Anthea.

"Totally... you're on your own. For the rest of your life... in your happiest moments, there's suddenly the thought people want you dead. And the media and cops would say I was low-life working at Pythons," said Liam.

"Not any more... it's destroyed," said Anthea.

"You said that."

Liam stayed quiet, trying to come up with something.

"I think Ithica's gone too," said Anthea. "Pete Jacobs is winning. He's catastrophically winning."

Anthea looked across at Liam. He was staring out the window. For no reason she was thinking of her previous attempts at suicide. She wondered which was greater: people trying to kill her or the number of times she'd thought about killing herself.

It was a human condition to try and survive. She was finding it increasingly impossible, though. The odds had always been against her. It was irrelevant she was a woman, though she questioned that sometimes when so many of her work colleagues wanted cock.

Thinking of more murders, her mind turned again to the secret Australian security lists she'd headed. Some of the brightest people in their fields were recruited, all made to work in isolation, sometimes for years, only to be killed or disappear when they finished or came to an abrupt halt. These people weren't spies; they were scientists, mathematicians, all brilliant in their fields. They had never wanted anything to do with Australian intelligence but were all forcibly threatened. Sometimes the threats were extended to their parents. Do this or your parents are dead.

Anthea saw each person on her list was driven to succeed. Working alone, they were more interested in achieving. Their belief being, through accomplishment, everything in their lives would fall into place. They were all so wrong.

There had been only five on her list, but one by one each person vanished. It had all been too easy. Their professional colleagues were afraid to speak up, worried the same may happen to them.

Anthea saw one day each person on her list was gone. Working separately, one of the five had achieved a desired result. His work was classified. It didn't make sense he was killed. He could have contributed more. He was tortured prior to his death. They hadn't trusted him and worried he had made an extra set of notes on his accomplishments. He died during the torture. His torture was filmed.

Then there were the other four on the list who were murdered. Her superiors were all paranoid and easily spooked. This was strange, given they were all spies. They were worried the four who hadn't succeeded were keeping information from them. All four were killed separately.

Anthea now saw another problem she hadn't seen before. She was thinking of people killed on the intelligence lists. It was a common thing but... the person managing the intelligence list was also killed.

All of these memories continually going over and over in her head. She knew it stopped her from thinking logically sometimes or slowed her thinking down.

A tear appeared in her left eye. She could feel it running down her cheek. Normally she ignored them. She knew what it meant. Tears from the right eye were joy. These were the usual sad tears. The perilous ones. It was part of her. Part of her human condition. It was all wrong.

When people knew she worked for intelligence there were always the questions of whether it was safe to sit or be seen with her. Would they be shot too?

"You're thinking of books and movies," she would automatically reply. "We disappear when nobody's looking."

It was true. At least at Ithica it was true. Anthea always said it stoically.

There was also no point having assets. At Ithica they were too tough to hang on to. It became worse with the arrival of Peter Jacobs. Agents at Ithica often woke to find the house or apartment they owned had been acquired by some clandestine company. There was nothing they could do except leave. There was no legal recourse. It was another reason most people working for Australian intelligence used the same real estate agency, accountants, and lawyers. Only to be destroyed.

Anthea had found this out the hard way when her former husband changed the contract details on their house to his.

Retirement wasn't going to happen. It wasn't an option. Dead was dead and gone.

Anthea had found it useless to even try to escape Australia. Instead she had gone to Carcoar.

Why had Liam appeared in her life? He too had good reasons to hate police and judges. What wasn't she seeing? She smiled when thinking of Liam. The boy was so well built. She'd seen him fucking everyone, including herself. How had that happened? If only he'd been sent to get her from Carcoar. She wouldn't have left. She would have stayed and had sex with him forever. What was happening? There was no way she was supposed to be happy. Why was he having sex with her? He was twenty-three years old.

It was now she noticed Shay appearing on her mobile.

"How long have you been there?" she asked.

Shay ignored Anthea's question. "Callam is gone—sorry, dead. He just died. People from Ithica... tortured him. It was barbaric. Human beings are such messy animals when it comes to tearing them apart."

Anthea said nothing. Her thoughts were coming very slowly.

"I'm still here, but I don't know for how long... You need to make decisions, Anthea," said Shay, now appearing on Liam's large television.

"I don't know how long I'll be able to help you before they destroy me... you're the last person remaining from Ithica. What do you want to do?" asked Shay.

Anthea looked across at Liam, who was now looking at Shay.

"We need to leave," said Anthea.

"Ok... ok... we can go to Timothy's farm," said Liam.

"Definitely not," said Anthea. "You'll spend all day fucking. It's not the answer."

"Then what Shay?" asked Liam, touching his groin.

Anthea shook her head.

"Guys, we're trying to stay alive," said Anthea.

"They know we're here... it's just a matter of when they arrive," said Shay.

"How do you know?" asked Liam. "They let me go."

"How can you be so blasé?" said Anthea.

"Guys... we don't have time for this. With Callam gone I'm supposed to vanish too. Anthea, choose somewhere. I don't know if you can rely on me for much longer. You have to do something."

Chapter 15
Kirsty

"They're your friend and still alive?" questioned Liam. "How did that happen, Anthea?"

The question wasn't funny. Liam's comment upset Anthea. She wouldn't react. She'd grown used to people around her dying. No... that was total lies. She'd never got used to it. She hoped one day somehow all the murders would be investigated. That wouldn't happen. People like Anthea had been jailed or killed trying to expose the murders.

"What did you say?" asked Anthea. "What did you ask?"

"Your friend Kirsty, how is she still alive?" asked Liam.

"She moved to California," responded Anthea. "She had to. But she's by no means safe over there."

"Australian intelligence have killed Australians overseas... I'd rather we didn't have this conversation now, Liam. Just be careful. Kirsty's a magician. Mainly Vegas. We went to uni together. I come here to hide when all else fails," said Anthea.

"You're here often?"

"Ha ha," Anthea said sarcastically. "It feels like you're picking on me. I just rescued you."

"Sorry, it's too much to take in. I wasn't picking on you. It's all too weird... Pythons gone. Callam's gone," said Liam.

"I don't work for Australian intelligence... and they want me dead... I don't know how you do it, Anthea..."

"You'll need to be careful, Liam. That's why we've come to Kirsty's. We should be safe here," said Anthea.

"Should be safe. You talk as though we're hiding from mafia or drug gangs."

Liam stood looking at the house and gardens while Anthea tapped on a hidden keypad to the left of the front door. Neat and tidy, the large dark brick bungalow was surrounded by landscaped grounds with tall oak trees dominating the block of land. Liam thought views of Sydney Harbour might be visible from the upper floor.

"You need to come inside, Liam," said Anthea. "I told you, Kirsty's a magician. She collects... and don't touch anything. It might be dangerous."

Anthea watched Liam walking around the large dimly lit room, waiting for questions. It was an Aladdin's cave of magician's apparatus, posters, and artwork Kirsty had collected over many years.

"I said don't touch... Liam," Anthea yelled, seeing Liam had a long sword in his hand.

Liam looked at her in defiance.

"Drop it. The last two people to withdraw that sword from its plinth had their right hand cut off. I'm not joking."

"How?"

"Kirsty's a magician... magic..."

"But they're just tricks... Can I sit in this chair?" said Liam, pointing to the chair in front of him.

"No... Not that chair... sit in the chair next to it."

"You've got to be kidding."

"I got Kirsty the chair from Ithica. It kills people. It was her going-away present."

"That's ridiculous... You're making this crap up to make me look silly."

"I'm not."

"You're telling me you gave your best friend a chair that could kill them... your best friend... and your intelligence agency built the chair... don't they have anything better to do? What other furniture do they make?"

"Now you're sounding silly," said Anthea.

"Why are you getting mad?"

"I'm trying to keep you alive," said Anthea.

"There's no doors," said Liam. "Where are the doors?"

"The front door."

"Yeah, but apart from that one... and the front door's gone," said Liam, surprised, looking at where they had entered.

"Take the seat cushion from that chair," Anthea said, pointing at a particular chair, "and throw it on the chair I said will kill you."

Liam was hesitant.

"Are you sure?"

Anthea nodded.

"You haven't got the wrong chair?"

"Don't do it then."

"What about that sofa? Can the two of us sit there? I just want to sit on something."

"We can sit here," said Anthea, pointing to the sofa in front of her.

"And it's safe for me to get there?"

"Yes. But touch nothing."

Liam hesitantly walked to the sofa. By the time he reached it, Anthea was already sitting there. It gave him some confidence knowing she was sitting there.

"Have you ever noticed how complicated your life is, Anthea?" asked Liam.

"I try not to," responded Anthea.

"Incredible... I think it's to do with intelligence... the agency... not yours... like really."

"I couldn't say."

"Exactly. Intelligence has all control... and then they get rid of you."

Anthea wondered if Liam was asking not to see her anymore.

"After my parents were murdered I tried to have a simpler life. Go to uni. Settle down... pole dancing..." said Liam.

Yes, it seemed like that. Her life was too complicated for him. Next she'd be hearing let's just be friends or being ghosted. She had to persuade him to change his mind.

"Didn't you find surviving at Pythons difficult?" she asked.

"We didn't know what was happening. We weren't told. But now you say Pythons is gone and Ithica... and some judges... They've wiped out an Australian intelligence agency and nobody noticed. You have to question if it was really needed," said Liam.

Anthea found the need to change subjects again.

"Kirsty likes to relax here."

"But most of Kirsty's stuff could kill you."

"I know, it's strange."

"And no doors... how do I get to a bathroom or anywhere else? Is there a bathroom?"

"Of course there's a bathroom. It's..."

Anthea was immediately quiet when she saw a man in a white suit now standing at the end of the room. He slowly walked towards them. Taking off his white jacket, his tight-fitting white shirt revealed his buff upper body. The thin tight fabric of his trousers showed the rest. Anthea looked across to see Liam.

"Friend of yours?" she asked.

"Give me time," said Liam.

The two watched as the stranger threw his white suit coat onto a magic stage prop. Landing on the prop, it was immediately catapulted into a large fish tank full of water. Anthea watched the suit coat be eaten by the water. She looked at Liam, who hadn't taken his eyes off the stranger.

"I'd offer you a chair but it could kill you," said Liam.

"I prefer to remain erect," the man said in what sounded like a Texan drawl.

"I'm imagining that."

Anthea looked closely at the man in front of her. Obviously, intelligence. Perhaps in his early forties. Perhaps American, but she wasn't totally convinced by the drawl. He hadn't reacted at all to the loss of his suit coat. She was curious as to how he'd got in.

"Anthea, we need to talk," he said.

"And if I don't want to?" responded Anthea.

"Look, Duchess, you'll like what I'm offering."

Anthea studied the guy further. He seemed like a B-grade actor. He was trying to be somebody. Very little made sense.

"You've got some front," Anthea said jokingly. The guy's crotch was too obvious.

"Some say a lot, but I know you'll like why I'm here. You will too, Liam."

"You know me?" questioned Liam.

"We've met."

"Where? Who?"

"Work it out. You're a big boy."

"That card table over there is safe," Anthea said, pointing to a dimly lit area. "Let's see what you've got."

"I need a bathroom," said Liam.

"Walk over there towards the small painting of the waterfall. The door will open," said the man. "That's correct, isn't it, Duchess?"

Anthea nodded.

"How do you know that?" questioned Liam.

"A magician never tells."

"But—"

"Are you pissing here or in the bathroom?" asked Anthea, looking at Liam.

Liam adjusted his groin as he stood. His erection was obvious.

"Bathroom."

Anthea looked at the man while the two sat down at the card table.

"Your people didn't give you a name?"

"Isn't needed. Some people might think they're at the top of the tree, but I look down on them and know they're not."

"And Pete Jacobs?" asked Anthea.

"On the nose... you got it in one."

"You're an overseas agency?"

"A concerned citizen."

"How concerned?" asked Anthea.

"I'm here. The two Jacobs have to go. Australian intelligence needs reining in. Too much power for our liking. You understand?"

"Depends who you are," said Anthea, though still reluctant to believe everything he was saying.

"Carcoar's pleasant this time of year... but you wouldn't have noticed... hiding in that shed."

"How does everyone know I hid in Carcoar? Was there a billboard?"

"You should see the bathroom," said Liam upon returning. "Fucking magic. It's like a ride in there. I'm going back for more—and the walls!"

"Not now," said Anthea.

Liam sat between the two of them.

"Shay's not here so you'll have to tell him," said the man.

"Shay?" responded Anthea.

"Yes."

"What do you know about Shay?"

"Let him know, just because Callam's dead he's not necessarily disappearing."

"Not necessarily?" asked Anthea.

"Being simple AI, he'll probably just become obsolete... like people."

"Terrific," said Anthea.

Anthea also noticed the guy's right leg was now touching Liam's leg. Liam was cock-focused, easily distracted.

"So what are you suggesting?" Anthea asked firmly.

"Yes," said Liam.

"I think you'll like part of this," the man said, now looking at Liam. "Tomorrow, 4 pm, we've organised for Pete Jacobs to attack and try to kill you in this house."

"I hope that's not the part I'll like," said Anthea.

"Well it is actually, because we'll be here to destroy him."

"How many tablets are you on?"

"What do you mean? None."

"Well that's the first problem."

"You have to understand—"

"Look, okay, I get the picture," Anthea interrupted. "You're sitting on the top of a pine tree screwing around. You take a Janet flight out to Australia."

"It's much more secret than Janet," he said trying to interrupt.

"And arrive here to fuck up some Australian intelligence agencies. You expect people to take notice of you. You're not saying who you are, who you work for, what your name is, or who'll be helping you."

"Yes."

"Okay, I'm completely sold," Anthea said jokingly.

"I'm not," said Liam.

"See? And that's Liam thinking with his cock."

"We have a problem," said the guy.

"Okay, and I'm just going to call you Dickhead to make it easier," said Anthea.

"It's Davos."

"Of course it is."

"Careful."

"Why? You can have me destroyed."

"Quiet, you two," said Liam. "Give Dick a chance."

"Thanks, Liam. You're right," said Davos, winking.

Anthea watched Davos's hand drift towards Liam's crotch.

"I know Jacobs is out of control but it's our place to stop him," said Anthea.

"But you're not," said Davos. "You're not stopping the AI juggernaut."

Anthea refused to admit it.

"I won't be here when Jacobs arrives," said Anthea.

"You have to be," said Davos.

"No, I don't."

Davos stared sharply at Anthea. All three were surprised when a pinball machine sprang to life. Then a juke box.

Anthea stood to turn them off but both immediately stopped.

"Weird," said Liam.

"Coincidence," said Anthea.

Then a cuckoo clock chimed four times.

"Four times." said Davos.

More calamity followed when a giant sword fell from a sculpture above the sofa Anthea and Liam had been sitting on.

"I was sitting there," said Liam.

"Yes, but you aren't now," said Anthea.

Davos remained silent.

"You said you were here before." said Anthea to Davos.

"No... No... I said I know where the bathroom is... That's all."

"We're going," said Anthea looking at Liam. "This way."

Liam was repositioning his erect cock as he stood.

"Careful," said Anthea leading Liam past the sword and sofa.

"You need to keep up," said Anthea now walking towards a large mirror. A panel to the left opened revealing a winding corridor. It was dark and Anthea used the torch on her mobile to proceed.

"Most people are happy to just have rooms in their houses," said Liam.

"I know, but keep moving," said Anthea.

"I am, I'm following you."

"Keep up," said Anthea coming to a T intersection and turning to the left.

"How do you know it's the left?" asked Liam.

"Kirsty was always left out."

Liam now noticed Anthea counting tiny bricks making up the walls.

"Why all the confusion?" asked Liam.

"To protect her... sixteen, seventeen."

"From what... who...?" asked Liam.

"Another time... keep walking," said Anthea. "we can only spend so much time in these two corridors otherwise."

"Otherwise?"

"They flood," said Anthea.

Walking a few steps more Anthea said "open Swiss" and both Liam and Anthea watched an entrance to another room suddenly appear. Anthea watched Liam's reaction.

It was like walking onto a stage. The timber floor boards, high ceiling, theatrical lights. A magic stage. And doors, all different sizes and finishes. As if suspended in space.

"They all say stage door," said Liam.

"At first they do... They change," said Anthea.

"Is it safe?" asked Liam.

"Yes..." said Anthea sitting down on a sofa. "All the rooms are . . . except for the front parlor. Davos can't get us here."

Liam cuddled up next to Anthea.

"If Kirsty has to have guests here, the front parlor is the only room they see. That and the bathroom," said Anthea.

"Never here, nor any of the other rooms?" asked Liam.

"No one sees the rest of her house... No one... Except me... And now you."

"It makes me feel special," said Liam.

"Good," said Anthea.

The two looked at each other. Anthea waited for Liam to speak first. She could tell he was trying to cope with everything.

"Why are you helping me?"

"I thought that was obvious," said Anthea gently.

I'm glad... when you're around... Usually it's saving my life though."

"I won't always be doing that."

"I know... what you mean," said Liam.

"I wish Shay was here. Even if he does always turn up at the wrong times. So much for being a mentor... No wonder Callam's gone."

"Hay... Callam was my friend too."

"I know... I know... " said Anthea.

"Do you think Pete Jacobs will win?"

"I hope not... It shouldn't even be a question... It shouldn't be possible... but... we can't have this conversation..."

"Why...? Why not..?" asked Liam now rolling over onto his chest and kissing and licking Anthea's upper leg. Getting higher. Somehow he was naked. When did that happen?. Anthea hadn't noticed.

"You and you're mouth," said Anthea staring at Liam body. "You can think about sex now?"

"You could too. Try... It's my default position... You said what's happening is out of your hands," said Liam now removing Anthea's clothes.

"You're in control here... I'm only doing what you want." said Liam.

Anthea could feel Liam's erect cock rubbing her leg while he slowly licked her...

"Shay...? How long have you been here?" she asked.

"Enough to hear I always turn up at the wrong times."

Shay was now fully visible on both Liam and Anthea's mobiles and a large television screen. Liam hadn't stopped.

"Can you do something else besides watch?" asked Anthea.

"Why?" asked Shay.

Anthea put her head back on the cushions and tried to ignore Shay. She tried to concentrate on Liam who was now. What is he doing?

Chapter 16
Power

Sleep is often the period when the body and mind rest. But not tonight.

Lying on the sofa with Liam, her mind turned to its subconscious. It too was trying to keep Anthea alive—and having a hard time of it.

Bombarded with the most brightly coloured images it could muster, in the hope Anthea might notice and see their significance. The mind is only capable of so much, though.

Anthea's dream centred on a narrow stream twisting through rolling green fields filled with bright flowers of every kind.

Everything was bright and happy. Anthea hadn't seen bright and happy for a long time, so she didn't recognise it.

She could see a small girl playing with a black-and-red wriggling stuffed toy. No—she was wrong. The toy was an actual small snake. The child was laughing.

Anthea wondered why the toddler wasn't scared.

"Ha ha ... ha. It tickles. Don't do that. It tickles, no ... don't bite," said the child.

The snake had grown a lot since Anthea first saw it. The two were playing again.

"You're getting fat," said the child, now standing but struggling to pick up the snake, which was now quite long and thick. Anthea didn't fear for the child.

It was the noise that bothered her. High-pitched. It was shaking her. No—the shaking was from Liam.

"I can't turn off my phone," said Liam.

"It's making a lot of noise," said Anthea.

"It's Davos," said Liam.

"Sorry to wake you lovebirds. I'm annoyed you think I'm a loser," said Davos, who had selected the video option for the call.

"It's four am," said Anthea. "You said Jacobs is turning up at four pm."

"Yes, but you doubt me. You think I'm capable of nothing. It's not true."

"OK," said Anthea, unhappy that Liam had taken the video call from Davos.

"And I can show you."

"Show us what?" said Liam.

"I've brought three Australian banks down. Froze their systems. No one can access their accounts."

"Which banks?" asked Liam.

"I head an international intelligence agency," said Davos

"A nameless agency," said Anthea. "Who has attacked three Australian banks and frozen their banking operations. Every intelligence agency will be interested in you now."

"You don't understand. Jacobs has too much power. He has to be taken down. It's for the greater good."

"Since when has intelligence been interested in the greater good? It has the short-sightedness of a three-toed sloth," said Anthea.

"You're wrong," said Davos.

"You've just frozen three banks. That's a lot of unhappy Australian intelligence people," said Anthea.

"You can't blame me for that," said Davos.

"Of course not. You take the blame for nothing. And I doubt you're clever enough to hide the origins of what you've done. It all leads back to you."

Davos's face tried to remain unemotional, but it also went pale.

"I think Pete Jacobs will be arriving before four pm, unless you go elsewhere and he finds you there ..." said Anthea.

"My agency knows where I am. They'll rescue me."

"They're not here now. Your number two is about to become number one," said Anthea.

"He's an idiot."

"More the reason he's not going to rescue you."

"I have to be going."

"I take it your main interest is hiding from Pete Jacobs now rather than destroying him."

"Other more important things have emerged."

"Your survival," said Anthea.

Davos ended the mobile conversation.

Anthea and Liam had remained lying on the sofa when Davos appeared. Both had been naked. Davos, by comparison, had been wearing new shimmering clothes made from the same fabric as his first white outfit. All revealing—at times too much.

"That guy is such a cock," said Liam.

"Like really," said Anthea. "I could see you in his white outfit."

"You prefer me in clothes?"

"I didn't say that," said Anthea, responding and moving towards Liam. The two kissed.

"Just the two of us," said Liam.

Anthea smiled. She wondered what Liam was thinking at that moment. No—she didn't want to know. She was pleased it was just the two of them and not sharing him with others at the club.

When had they last eaten? They hadn't.

She tried not to think about Ithica. It was impossible.

"So we can move anywhere we like now," said Liam.

"What?" said Anthea.

"Ithica's gone. Pythons ... we don't have to stay in Sydney."

"I can't leave now," said Anthea. "I can't. People have been killed for no reason. Australians need to know."

"Can't someone else do it?" asked Liam.

"They've all been killed trying," said Anthea.

"I used to hear those stories at Pythons," said Liam. "One night, there were four of us. Upstairs, in one of the newly renovated suites...

The entire bedroom was a wet area. Hand cut Moroccan mosaics and specialty Italian marble. It had a dry sauna."

"Liam. Stop with the gay decorating gene," complained Anthea.

'Just setting the scene... One of the guys was complaining all his friends were disappearing. He was afraid he'd be next. He broke down completely and wept... Hanging on to me and crying... He couldn't go to military counselling... He'd end up in a psych ward or disappear... He told me after we'd had sex. Just the two of us... "

Liam saw Anthea was rolling her eyes.

"No it really was just the two of us. One minute he was feeling euphoric after sex with me and the next he was crying his eyes out.

"I'll remember that the next time we're having sex," said Anthea.

"You were the same. We had sex and the next minute you're telling me you couldn't have sex or see me again... because of your job, your age and everything else. We'd already had sex five times by then."

"I was just making it clear."

"And Callam ... you kept saying you wanted to see Callam, not me." said Liam.

"Yeah, well, that was harder than I thought it would be—ended up going home with you instead," said Anthea.

"Well Callam's dead. He's gone. I know he helped you a lot. He helped me too. I loved him."

Anthea was caught out by Liam's response.

"I just wish people would stop disappearing," said Anthea.

"We've both had dreadful times, babe ... I think I burnt the bridges with the judges," said Liam.

"Because they tried to kill you?" said Anthea.

"Yes...That too."

"Babe, you need to stop thinking about everything that's happening," said Anthea.

Anthea saw Liam was holding the base of his erect cock.

"Can I interest you in coming back to bed?" asked Liam.

"I'm worried. And serious. And you're being so Mills and Boon," said Anthea.

"I was going for Falcon Studios," said Liam.

"They're all gay men."

"And ... you like watching them," said Liam.

Anthea clambered along the bed and lay next to Liam.

"We're in the same boat," said Liam.

"Is it sinking?" asked Anthea.

"Definitely," said Liam. "You can't beat intelligence. Especially when they say it's in the interests of national security."

"Oh yes, that old chestnut," said Anthea.

"Who are you talking about now?" asked Liam.

"The old chestnuts," said Anthea.

"You're saying that and playing with my balls. I'm getting confused... and more aroused," said Liam.

"They want you to be confused."

"My balls?" asked Liam.

"Australian intelligence."

"Are we still on them?" asked Liam.

"They're gaining more power, destroying more Australians."

"We both know that. But there's nothing we can do. Only run away," said Liam.

" I have to try Liam," said Anthea.

"Was Joan of Arc your favourite bedtime story at school?" asked Liam.

"No. Growing up in orphanages and home care, I tried to imagine a better life."

As soon as she said it, Anthea realised it was wrong. She'd said too much. It had become her default—having a worse backstory than the people around her. It was attention-seeking, and this time she regretted it. Liam already knew about her childhood, and she knew about his.

She could have easily just said no and left it at that. Liam was joking, but she'd taken it seriously.

"You're right. Joan was my poster child."

"It's time we changed your posters," said Liam.

"I wish it was that easy," said Anthea. "I really do."

"It can be," said Liam. "Why don't you hang on to this joystick? You can fly wherever you want ... but save the world another day ... the world can wait."

Anthea followed her pilot's orders. It was a two-hour flight. After which they both fell asleep, exhausted.

"Anthea ... Anthea ... you need to be awake ... you need to see this," yelled Shay on Anthea's mobile.

"Is it breakfast?"

"No. It's Davos. He's been found dead on the steps of the Supreme Court."

"A bit theatrical," said Liam.

"Yes, so the police moved Davos down the street to the front of an office building."

"The police moved the body?"

"Yes. Officially the media's reporting he died out the front of an office building."

"So they changed crime scenes?"

"And the police are saying it's suicide. No suspicious circumstances."

"Of course there isn't. They created the crime scene."

"And Davos was his real name," said Shay.

"That's what the police are telling us. We still don't know what agency he's from. Australian or overseas? How many aliases does he have?"

"He's overseas. He's intel across a number of agencies. The police are having a tough time. They just want him to disappear," said Shay.

"Then they should have done that instead of creating the crime scene," said Anthea.

"The police were told to move Davos for a reason. That's why he didn't disappear. They'll say he's an overseas visitor. Australian intelligence—or rather Pete Jacobs—is telling overseas agencies not to interfere," said Shay.

"He's at war with them now," said Anthea.

"Any chance of breakfast?" asked Liam.

"Yes," replied Anthea. "Australian media have reported Davos's death. They'll be told to drop the story now."

"You think he was sent to be killed?" asked Shay.

"Probably. But that shows you he's not from US agencies. They take their agents' lives seriously—not like Australia."

"Is there a kitchen?" asked Liam. "I can get something for us."

"Over there towards the stone wall," said Anthea. "Say bread. I'll just have grape juice."

"Like as in wine?" asked Liam. "I'll make something."

"Did you believe Davos when he said Jacobs will be here at four?" asked Shay.

"I don't know. I wanted to believe Davos when he said you'll be around for longer than you originally thought. You'll survive Callam," said Anthea.

"I don't understand how I'm still here," said Shay.

"Do you miss Callam? You were created for him," said Anthea.

"I certainly got to know everything about Callam. I could tell you what his reactions would be. What words he would use in his conversations. After a certain time—towards the end—I could tell what he was thinking despite all the possibilities. The amount he thought about me was huge. So was the amount he liked me. He called it love ..."

"Do you think you could have saved him?"

"If he wanted me to. But he didn't want to be saved."

Anthea saw what Shay was saying. She felt the need to help people, even if it killed her.

"I'm a bit like Callam," said Anthea.

"You're very similar to Callam. You both have the same destructive impulses."

Anthea was surprised. Shay was supposed to be Callam's mentor.

"Human beings are very simple creatures. You are ... easily persuaded and manipulated ... like, really. Your ideas on what's right and wrong ... all based on supposition. You think you've done well so far. Humans have this huge willingness to destroy others. You need us," said Shay.

"Can you really tell what I'm thinking now?"

"Your mind is really too jumbled and fragmented, Anthea. At the moment you can't tell me what you're thinking—how do you expect me to?"

"That's close enough," said Anthea.

"Liam's good for you."

"What?"

"Yes, he is. He's having you reassess your life. Get rid of this life-or-death condition. That's why we're having this conversation."

"Why?"

"Have you missed the first forty years of your life?"

"I'm thirty-eight."

"You're going to ask me what you should do next."

"Why would I do that?"

"Because you're unable to work it out yourself. You've botched it so many times."

"What do you need to know?"

"Nothing. I already know you, Anthea."

"I'll be straight back. I have to check on Liam in the kitchen," said Anthea.

"I can join you in the kitchen," said Shay.

"No ... no, no ... I don't want to worry Liam. I'll be back."

Anthea reached for an oversized T-shirt. While putting it over her head, she raced for the kitchen.

Liam was sitting on a stool. Still naked.

"Are you having it off with Shay?" asked Liam.

"Yeah ... I like plastic."

"Oooh, that hurts."

"What did you find to eat?"

"Dinosaur eggs and cupcakes ... and coffee. I made coffee with powdered milk. Lots of frozen and dried everything," said Liam.

"Coffee to go," said Anthea. "I have to rush back to Shay for a bit," she added, pouring the coffee and hurrying off.

"We can have the cupcakes when you get back. According to the packaging, they last seven years."

"Great," said Anthea. "I won't be long," she added, finding a hidden door back to Shay.

"I'm back," said Anthea, now turning her attention to Shay.

"Save me," she said, returning to the sofa, then looking at her mobile screen for Shay.

"Where are you?" asked Anthea.

"You won't be able to do it," said Shay.

Anthea looked seriously at him.

"From the beginning," said Anthea

"Later today, Davos said 4pm, Pete Jacobs is dropping by to kill you. Jacobs is punctual. He will be attending at 4. He is far superior to you and more powerful.

"I've survived his meetings in the past. I was his personal assistant."

"Yes, I remember that went well," Shay said sarcastically. "You escaped to spend three years in Carcoar wondering why you were still alive."

"I have to win. To beat Jacobs... otherwise. That's why I'm here," said Anthea.

"I'm AI. I can't believe in miracles and in these circumstances, it's better you don't either... Are you listening?"

Anthea heard the severity of what Shay was telling her. He wasn't saying she'd definitely die."

"So I have to escape now?" she said.

"I didn't say that. Not at all. You haven't gone through all of this to run away. Callam didn't bring you back to Ithica to have you killed."

"I'm not convinced of that. Are you sure?"

"He brought you back because he knew you could make a difference. I didn't see it," said Shay.

"You told him not too bring me back."

"Yes. I could see he would be killed. He should have taken off but he didn't. He wanted to spend time with his mates. It was his decision."

"You could have warned him."

"Like I'm warning you. I did."

"So why isn't he still alive?"

"Like I keep telling you Anthea. Because he wouldn't listen. Like you're not listening now."

"To what?" said Anthea striving hard to understand what Shay was saying.

"You have to trick Pete Jacobs. That's the only way."

"He's cleverer than me. You said that."

"Yes... He's cleverer than both of us together, but you have to trick him."

"Like magic?"

"I'll show you how. I'll train you."

Anthea felt more confused. "What trick?"

"We're only using words but you have to look extremely confident," said Shay. "but not overly confident."

"I look confident."

"No you look hopeless. Are we doing this or not? You're running out of time."

"If I don't?"

"He'll kill you... and definitely kill Liam as well... Intelligence agencies here and overseas will be watching. They need you to succeed."

Anthea felt immense strain on her shoulders and lower back. Shay said not to worry. Kills confidence and Jacobs would be picking that up. Her presentation had to be natural and authoritative. He had her repeat the same sentences over and over. Don't blink as often. Wear your hair back, but not so much that he notices. Smile but not too much. Put your hands here, then here, then back again. When you say particular words have your hands by your side. But not like that.

"Couldn't I just send you?" said Anthea after one of her many repeat performances.

"This is truly life and death Anthea... for you and Liam... the odds are greatly against you."

"Do you think it will work Shay?"

"My trick will work...it's whether you can carry it off... You'll only get one chance. You have to be ready."

Anthea remained silent.

"I'd pop back and see Liam if I was you. Don't tell him anything though. It's your battle. Not his."

Anthea returned to the kitchen to see Liam who was occupied with a PlayStation. As soon as he saw her he took his headphones off.

"Babe it's nearly four. What did Shay say?" he asked now standing in front of her.

"He said it should all be fine. I just have to do what he told me."

"And that's all?"

"That's the shortened version."

"What about Jacobs wanting you dead?"

"I haven't got time now."

"We can still run."

Anthea glanced at her watch.

"We've got forty three minutes. It's too late to run babe. As long as I do what Shay told me. It'll be fine."

"I put some cupcakes out for you. They've got fluro pink icing. The packaging says they last for seven years. There's stacks of them in what looks like a bakery room. For a person who doesn't live here there's an enormous amount of food. There's a walk in cool room and a three storey wine cellar. Three levels. And they're all full."

Anthea could see Liam was nervous. The chattering. She took one of the cupcakes.

"And the cool room has its own walk in section for ice wines. It's all huge," said Liam.

"I think it best you hide here when Jacobs comes. Say in the bakery room," said Anthea.

"The bakery?" replied Liam.

"I'll be seeing Jacobs in the front parlor," said Anthea.

"I'll go with you if you want me to."

"No you'll be safer here," Anthea said kissing Liam. What started as short kiss became a full-on mouth session."

Anthea finally escaped. Running to the door she could see Liam's image reflected in the mirror by the door. He was looking at her like a lost puppy. In the moment she thought she should have looked back but she didn't.

She was thinking about what Shay had told her. Her hands, be positive, affirmative, but not demanding. Hair.

She scoffed down the pink cupcake. It tasted surprisingly nice for something that would last seven years. She needed a drink. There was no time to go back to the kitchen. White wine would have to do.

Her mind was racing. Looking at her watch, she would have sworn the band was pink, not green. There was no time left. It was 3:50pm. The time had flown. She should be in the front parlor. Why was she feeling jittery, jumpy, nervous?. Jacobs wants to kill her. It's probably that. Does it matter? She didn't know.

"The front parlor," she said out loud.

"Here we go to the front parlor. Wish me luck, Kirsty," said Anthea wondering where to sit. "Should I sit or stand? Wait. Shay didn't tell me that. It's all right for him being naked on a screen. What will I do?"

She was perplexed. Should she sit or stand? Lie down? Possibly too casual. Hands. Hands. She'll sit on a chair. Which chair? Which chair was safe. There wasn't time to call Kirsty and ask where she should sit. She had to look relaxed when Pete Jacobs arrived. He could already be there.

Anthea wondered what was happening. Stress? It was Shay's fault. He could have handled this. If he was so perfect at it then he should be doing it. Telling me what I can't do isn't very positive. Especially when he said I'd be killed when I failed. Very negative.

"You can shove AI up your Pete Jacobs," said Anthea now seeing him before her.

"You look taller," she said staring at him confused.

"Unfortunately you're still alive Anthea," said Jacobs.

"Enough with the pleasantries Mr. Jacobs," said Anthea trying to understand what was happening in front of her. Jacobs was standing in a corner of the room. Her eyesight had become blurry. She couldn't be sure what she was seeing. Reluctant to say anything she stared at Jacobs.

"You have nothing to say?"

"Your teeth are falling out," she blurted out.

"Ridiculous."

"I know, but they are. There's another one. Can't you feel it?"

"I'm not listening."

"Well you should."

"Another," said Anthea. "This looks really bad," she added. Try to sound positive. Smile. No. Remember what Shay said. Why is there a large silver ball floating behind Jacobs? Don't panic. Stay... Stay calm. Control. Control. Control.

"But nothing excessive."

"What?" asked Jacobs.

"What what?" asked Anthea.

"You said nothing excessive."

"Yes," said Anthea moving her hands to be by her side then on her hips. Her right hand then touched her left ear before holding both hands together out the front. Look normal. She wondered if this is what Shay was talking about. Act firm and assertive. Don't show your scared but be a little afraid. It shows confidence.

Pete Jacobs seemed to be moving around the room. He had his hand up covering his mouth.

"I didn't think you'd turn up today."

"What?"

"Theres a large silver ball behind you. It looks as though it's going to drop on you."

Jacobs hesitated before saying. "No there isn't."

"Well I can see it. Why can't you?"

"It's not there. There's no ball there."

"Now it's a black frog."

"What black frog? I came here to kill you."

"But there's a huge black frog behind you."

"I can't see it. Did you hear me? I came to kill you."

"This is bigger than you. With everything happening. I'm surprised you showed up today," said Anthea. Look at his eyes. Don't stare. Move your shoulders but don't swing them. Tilt your head to the side. The right side. Not the left. Wait until he replies.

"What everything?"

"You're replacement." Say the sentence calmly. Naturally. Naturally in a European way. Not the Australian way with a lot of eucalyptus and wattle.

"I'm not being replaced." When he says I'm not being replaced. Put your lips together and frown. It's more difficult with Botox so clench your buttocks together at the same time as though you've got diarrhea. Count to two slowly and relax.

"Who are you?" It's imperative you keep to the script. Any divergence may result in your death.

"I'm serious Pete. I thought you would have been out of here after what Davos said last night."

"Who's Davos?"

"The guy you killed yesterday. No wonder they're replacing you."

"No one is replacing me." Jacobs said.

"You might want to check that. Davos said you're obsolete and high maintenance now. A little unstable. One AI company has created an upscale super computer and they're up and ready. I hear you haven't even got your own computer hub. You have to share."

"This isn't right."

"And at your age it's impossible to replace some of your broken parts. You're too old."

"You're wrong."

"I heard they were flicking the switch at 4pm today. I thought you'd be gone. Certainly not here. I'd be looking for power if I was you."

Stand firm with your legs slightly apart. Not too far apart. So you can fit a baseball between your legs at the level of your feet. Do not smile. Have your mouth closed and deep breath through your nose. Wait until Pete Jacobs has left. Do not act surprised and say nothing. Walk away.

Word of caution. If this doesn't go well. Jacobs will kill you. Anthea remembered all of this. Shay had taught her well. He didn't mention the silver ball, giant black frog, snakes, teeth, broken mirrors and all the dead birds though. And where was she?

Chapter 17
I Totally See

"Pump one, pump it again, pump it till it hurts. And spurl. More spurl. Breathe, stop breathing, pump. You're all doing well, feel it, feel it."

Anthea watched a semi-naked guy doing aerobic dance steps, his image projected onto a wall. Shay was visible on another equally large screen.

"I want to see those beats. Rub it till it's red ... and two, three, four, get the fifth one in. Stretch it, and shoot."

Watching the gym guy gyrate while Shay tried to follow on his screen, Anthea thought it weird. Liam was flapping around, falling down, maybe bruising himself, but seemingly not noticing.

"On your knees ... hunger, hunger, hunger ... swing those hips. You should be able to feel blood ... feel it ... and release. Keep breathing though ... now we're going to stand using the soles of our feet. Beat, step, beat. That's great, you're going well. And hole, star, hole ... star ... hold."

Confused, Anthea was interested in where this was going. She wondered if the gym instructor was AI. Shay seemed to be watching the instructor carefully, though listening to the instructor made no sense.

"Star star crabs, star star crabs, star ... now peddling. Peddling. I said peddling, not piddling. Peddling. No, clean up, you'll slip. Peddling. And spurl."

The instructor now turned his back to the cameras.

"See what I did there ... line, line, star ... sweat, sweat ... play it down ... get on your back. On your back ... you should be able to feel it at the back of your neck ... and now running down your neck ... try not to swallow ... swing those hips ... you should have hard nipples by now ... this is great for another area of your body ... and touch."

The music was now much louder. Shay was still dancing. His nipples and cock were erect, but that seemed normal. Liam was all over the place before collapsing on his back on the floor. Here he moved his arms and legs like a cockroach trying to roll over.

"Bring it in ... I don't know how many male ballet dancers are watching, but this next exercise is for you. Keep touching your nipples. More star, crutch, star. You may know the exercise. It's from the Karma Sutra."

Finding the remote, Anthea turned off the volume.

"What's happening?" said Liam, still struggling on his back.

Anthea sat down next to him. He seemed out of it, but so was she.

"Cupcakes."

"There's more on the bench," said Liam.

Anthea laughed. "I think they're drugged, laced with something."

"There's more there if you want some."

"No, it's fine," said Anthea.

"Where'd you go?" asked Liam.

Liam was more out of it than she thought.

"Went to see Jacobs. He dropped in ... but he had to run. Other agencies want him destroyed," Anthea said, keeping it light and breezy.

Liam was grappling with working out what was happening. Unable to fathom it, he gave up. She wasn't doing much better herself.

Shay was still working out, watching the instructor and trying to mimic him.

"Why's Shay working out?" Anthea asked Liam. "He's AI, for God's sake. Why the exercise?"

"Yeah," was Liam's reply.

Anthea reached for a cushion and lay next to Liam on the floor. Finally, time to relax. No — it was short-lived. Her phone was making another noise. She recognised it.

"Anthea Tonelli, is that you?" said a friendly-sounding man's voice on the phone. "Can you swipe your finger on the phone, then we can tell for sure?"

Anthea did as requested.

"That's terrific. This is just an update. You'll be glad to hear we're restructuring Ithica."

"It was obliterated, Sir."

"I heard that. I haven't worked for Ithica, but I hear you did ... did you know the name Pete Jacobs?"

Anthea was reluctant to say anything. Was this all a joke? The man hadn't said his name, rank, or any details.

"I'll be heading up Ithica," he said, not waiting for Anthea to reply.

"Congratulations, Sir," said Anthea. "Will we know your name, Sir?"

"Yes, you will. It has to be announced."

"Yes, of course, Sir," said Anthea, as if everything the man was saying made sense. None of it did though.

"You mightn't have heard this, but it seems Pete Jacobs was destroyed by other AI ... artificial intelligence ... I have to get up to speed on AI, but it seems Pete Jacobs got the better of Ithica just before he was destroyed."

"Really?" said Anthea, at the same time thinking they'd appointed this guy to ensure Ithica was obliterated again.

"Pete Jacobs has managed to entirely wipe out the reserves of the Defence Bank. Over four billion was taken."

"Four billion?" asked Anthea.

"Cleaned it out. Defence members don't know. Treasury is having to supply the bank with necessary day-to-day funds. We don't know how Pete Jacobs did it, but it seems he did the same for a few other government departments. I can't say which ones."

"But you said Jacobs is gone?," questioned Anthea.

"And so is the money."

"Sir, do you think you could tell me your name?" asked Anthea.

"I prefer to wait until it's announced. Do things officially. I don't like things to go wrong."

"Of course not, Sir."

"It's essential we do things by the book."

"Yes, that seems to work, Sir," said Anthea, sounding serious but wondering if the guy was for real. People were often promoted above their competence, but this was exceptional.

"Until I have more information, I have no idea what's happening."

"I totally see that, Sir," replied Anthea.

The unnamed man was gone. Anthea nestled in next to Liam.

"Did you hear any of that?" Anthea asked Liam.

"I was listening to the birds singing," responded Liam.

What birds singing, Anthea wondered, and looked at him. Liam was relaxed, lying on the floor — not waving his hands and legs around, but lying next to her. Anthea wished it were all that simple. But it never was. She only had to look at Shay to see that.

Instead of bouncing around trying to follow the instructor's moves, Shay was now in flight — floating through the air, leaping, turning, spinning.

The instructor had somehow seen Shay's movements and, not to be outdone, had attempted the same himself. It was naturally catastrophic. Surely the instructor had questioned Shay's appearance — totally naked and created by Callam to be the most beautiful man he would ever see.

But no.

The instructor crashed to the ground on the first leap — floating through the air only to discover ... gravity. Recovering? Hardly. Again, not to be outdone, the instructor watched Shay spiralling upwards before splaying his legs to land. Easy enough if you're AI and ground level is when and wherever you want it to be. Ruinous and damaging if you're human.

Shay watched the instructor now feebly attempting the easiest of floor movements. The cavorting was gone. He looked to be in pain doing some of the most basic stuff — like being on his knees and bent forward.

Shay lost interest. His large projection was gone and instead he occupied Anthea's mobile screen.

"I saw and overheard the phone call," said Shay to Anthea.

"I'm glad, because I didn't believe it," responded Anthea.

"Oh — and Kirsty is about to arrive here."

Anthea was excited. "That's great news," she told Shay.

It was a lie, though.

Kirsty always had a habit of showing up when Anthea was enduring the worst of times. Somehow Kirsty knew. The exception was Carcoar. It had all happened so quickly — the fire, trapped in her panic room. It became a death trap. If the fire hadn't killed her, the water, gas, and flames would have. Escaping and homeless, she had spent the first couple of days sleeping under the railway arches in Wentworth Park. Years later she heard she had died in the fire. The authorities even identified her.

"She's here," said Shay.

Liam was still lying on the floor. Anthea left him there and went to the front parlour.

Kirsty walked in. Entrances were her specialty.

"Couture ... what have they done to you?" asked Anthea. "I mean, wow," she said, running to her.

"I brought you some," said Kirsty, wrapping her arms around Anthea, who was careful not to crush any of Kirsty's clothes — cashmere, silk, and pink diamonds.

"Thanks, Kirsty. I'm glad you're here."

"You are not," said Kirsty. "But more of that later. I need to change. Do you want to take a bath with me?"

"Next time," said Anthea. "This is Shay," she added, showing Kirsty her mobile phone face.

"He's naked ..."

"Well, yes ..."

"This is the guy you're seeing?" quizzed Kirsty, looking at Anthea's phone.

"No, no," said Anthea, laughing. "I'm not seeing Shay."

"Anthea, have a bath with me. We can talk. I renovated. You haven't seen my new bathroom, but neither have I. It's the size of a basketball court."

Anthea was intrigued. "OK ... OK."

The world had stopped. Anthea had taken off her clothes and sat on the edge of a large soapy pool.

"Jump in the bath," said Kirsty.

Anthea remained sitting on the edge, looking at the new world around her, questioning what was happening, doubting it was real — still wondering if she was hallucinating. How? Worried she would see more large silver balls or other objects.

The small tiles were heated, soft to touch. The light was fresh, pink. The water was warm. It flowed and spouted from all parts of the room, showering down and splashing into pools.

"Swim over here, Anth. It's warmer," said Kirsty.

Anthea immersed herself in the water. It felt different — lighter, fluffier, even without soap suds. She looked up at the coffered ceilings, flying buttresses, and columns.

It seemed "if in doubt, throw it in" was the architectural style, but Anthea would keep that to herself.

The two women were now sitting opposite each other. Anthea waited for Kirsty to speak first. Why was Kirsty here now? She only returned to Australia when something was wrong.

"I've got a break between shows. Launching a new magic show next month. They tell me bookings are terrific. It's three shows a day, six days a week."

Anthea knew that wasn't the reason Kirsty returned.

"This is beautiful. Better than any retreat," responded Anthea.

Kirsty leaned towards her and whispered into her ear.

"They ransacked my home in Vegas."

"Who's they?"

"Your mob. We have it all on tape. The casino's furious. They're supposed to have the best security. It was a walk-in — took jewellery, gold, bank account information — and they want more."

"How do you know it was Australian intelligence?"

"They left a thank-you card."

"Saying what?"

"Anthea and Pete Jacobs thank you ... it's as though you're married to him."

"And what's the casino doing?" asked Anthea.

"I spoke to Glutes. He said the casino's doing an examination."

"What does that mean?"

"I have no idea Anthea. Glutes said other people at the casino are having cash problems besides me."

"That's because it's a casino," said Anthea.

"They're looking after me. They put me on one of their private jets and sent me here to relax."

"So they got rid of you."

Kirsty now looked worried. She had no idea what was happening. Anthea felt afraid too. She'd only known a small fraction of what Pete Jacobs was doing.

"My savings and investments — I'm totally exposed," said Kirsty, standing naked on the bath seat in front of Anthea.

"That's true, perhaps you could sit down," Anthea quickly replied, not wanting to see ...

"Oh ... the casino's blaming you," said Kirsty while moving carefully to sit on the seat. In the bubbles she could only feel around.

"What for?"

"For Jacobs," replied Kirsty.

Anthea froze in the warm water. Everything had suddenly blown up. Jacobs hadn't just been destroying agencies and authorities in Australia — he'd been doing the same overseas.

"Your casino knows we're friends?" asked Anthea.

"Friends steal a lot from their friends ... those are their words."

"But Jacobs is gone. He's ... was ... AI ... he was destroyed this afternoon."

"Convenient," said Kirsty. "If you read that in a book, you wouldn't believe it."

"Hey ... he was. Davos came to destroy Jacobs."

"Where's Davos from?"

"He wouldn't tell us."

"Well, he will now."

"No. He's dead."

"Anthea, you're not helping. Is everyone around you dead or naked like Shay?"

Anthea remained silent. It seemed the answer was yes. Worse still, she didn't know how much trouble Jacobs had caused. She assumed she would find out when she returned to Ithica — if she did.

"They're reforming Ithica," said Anthea to Kirsty, who by this time was looking at her face in a mirror.

"Why?"

"I don't know, but the guy who's replacing Jacobs called me today. Didn't tell me his name, but —"

"He didn't tell you his name ... but said he's going to be your boss?"

"He said Jacobs had stolen four billion from the Defence Bank. I didn't tell you that, though," said Anthea.

"And it's got yours and Jacobs' names all over it."

"My name's only on the stuff Jacobs took from you," said Anthea.

"And the other people he ripped off in Vegas," added Kirsty.

"You didn't tell me that."

"I've got an underground bunker here. You might want to use it."

Anthea remembered her hideaway at Carcoar. It was all sickening.

"It's luxurious like this. It can accommodate ten people," said Kirsty.

"You try to save me every time," said Anthea.

"I know."

"I'll find your stuff when I return to Ithica. Also, Shay can help me."

Kirsty was now reclining on a semi-submerged waterbed.

"The casino will contact you," said Kirsty.

"It's better if they don't. I'll be able to get your stuff back faster ... hopefully," added Anthea.

"Will we go back and see Liam?" asked Anthea.

"Yes, please. I'm surprised he didn't join us," said Kirsty.

Anthea smiled. Behind the smile, though, was a lot of confusion. Why would Liam join them? Kirsty had said she wanted to talk to her ... alone. The two of them were naked. Had Liam joined them. Anthea knew what would happen. Liam would be wanting sex.

Performing in Vegas, Kirsty was manicured, coiffured to an amount Anthea didn't know possible. Even her speech was tailored. Each word sounded crisp. Her sentences succinct. Her smile and laugh. Anthea remembered what they used to be — nothing like the current.

Was she jealous?

Yes ... terribly.

She didn't do jealousy. It was life-destroying, and in her job ... well, her job was life-destroying.

Kirsty was again standing naked on the side of the pool, her body taut. Picking up a rolled towel from a side table, Kirsty made it look like ballet.

Was it better if Liam didn't meet Kirsty? No. It would happen anyway. She'd better get it over with.

The configuration of Kirsty's home was confusing. Anthea had very little idea of its many secret doors and passages. Yes, every room was concealed — but where? Kirsty had even designed round rooms, and some revolved.

Walking into the kitchen area again, Liam was balancing on his head, wearing only a baggy pair of shorts. Shay was edging him on from a large screen.

Anthea saw Kirsty immediately looking at Shay — his cock flying from side to side.

Liam stopped as soon as he saw Kirsty.

"You must be twenty-three-year-old Liam," said Kirsty.

"I am," said Liam.

"Good guess," said Anthea.

Wearing a very baggy pair of silk shorts, it was easy to see what Liam wasn't hiding.

"I need to shoot ... and get some more clothes," said Liam.

Anthea was smiling. It was obvious Liam had another erection.

"Can I give you a hand?" said Anthea hurriedly, thinking Kirsty might get in first. No — that was silly. She was overthinking. Her friend had only just arrived ... to tell her she'd been wiped out in Vegas by Jacobs and Anthea was getting the blame.

"No, it won't take long. You need to catch up with Kirsty. I'm sure there's plenty to talk about."

Anthea was about to walk with Liam to the front door when her mobile rang. It was the same number as last time — supposedly her new boss.

"Is that Anthea Tonelli?"

"Yes," said Anthea, wondering what problems had happened.

"Ithica is to be set up in temporary offices, and I need you to report tomorrow morning at 8 am. They're installing everything now."

"Can you tell me the location, and do you have a name yet?"

"Yes to the first and no to the second," said the man, then immediately ended the call.

"Everything all right?" enquired Kirsty.

"Yes, smooth," said Anthea, before her mobile rang again.

"Is that Anthea Tonelli?"

Anthea recognised the voice and put the mobile on speaker.

"Yes, it is, but understandably, if you can't tell me who you are, then I'm ending this call."

"I can't, but I can tell you the location of Ithica's temporary offices."

"No ... there's such a thing as a flow of information even in intelligence — even Australian intelligence. You'd be having me walk into the unknown."

"I'm on a steep learning curve here."

"That's your choice, not mine," said Anthea.

"I'm your superior."

"With no name."

"Look ... I'm looking at Ithica, and it has an extraordinarily substantial number of employees. I've counted nearly two thousand. That's not the reason I've taken the job though — so it looks good on my résumé, I think ..."

"Sorry to interrupt, Sir, but when you've got some information to tell us which isn't classified or top secret — like your name — then we could all meet, and you'll see how many employees there are."

"That's what I was about to say ... I'm lodging an official formal complaint about you, Anthea Tonelli," the man said, before ending the call.

"Who's the crazy guy?" Shay asked, having overheard the call.

"He won't tell me — except he says he's the new head of Ithica."

"I wouldn't rush there if I were him. I'd be running away," said Shay.

"I would too," said Anthea.

"An official formal complaint ... is he serious? He hasn't even got an office yet," said Shay.

"What are you going to do, Anthea?" asked Kirsty. "You can always come back to Vegas with me."

"Your casino would arrest me. I'd end up in jail."

Chapter 18
Top Down

The new head of Ithica claimed to be Bram Hilderman, but Shay had dug around. A few missions overseas had forced Bram to urgently move countries, change his name, and alter his appearance. The alternatives were incarceration or being killed.

No, it wasn't spy stuff — saving lives and countries. It was distributing drugs through diplomatic channels and incompetence on a massive scale. Whoever was protecting Bram was surely wondering why.

Anthea was commanded to appear at Ithica's new temporary offices at HMAS Kuttabul. Arriving at the navy base, she was taken to the tri-service munitions compound.

"This is strictly temporary," said Bram, ignoring the usual pleasantries and instead voicing what he was thinking as he looked at her.

Looking around, Anthea could see very few munitions. There was a lack of bullets, very few guns, no rocket launchers.

"What happened? Was everything stolen?" she joked to Bram.

"You heard," said Bram.

"Yes," said Anthea. She hadn't, but it would give her an edge over Bram.

"Are all employees at Ithica this lax? Does everyone arrive late?"

"I'm the only one left, Sir."

"That's ridiculous. I've looked. Ithica has a staff of two thousand. Quite a few are being paid a lot more than me. I checked — you aren't one of them."

"That's according to records, Sir. The actual number is far smaller."

"That's nonsense, and I'll have none of it. You know what they say about conspiracy theories?"

"They have theories on conspiracy theories, Sir."

"Yes — no. There's no such thing as a conspiracy theory. You simply don't have all the facts."

"It's a good theory, Sir, but what if the facts aren't the actual facts?"

I haven't got time for stupidity. I'll get rid of the lot of them."

"The government's already done that, Sir."

"Ridiculous."

"Sir, if you might listen. Twenty people worked for Ithica before it was obliterated. Two thousand people were on the payroll."

"Ridiculous."

"I totally agree, Sir. You're dealing with a lot of skulduggery here. Could I advise you to tread carefully — for both our sakes?"

"This is hopeless. I'm having to deal with this mess because you failed to take care of it before I arrived."

Anthea shouldn't have been surprised by what Bram said. Bram was here for an easy time. Nothing to see on his watch.

"Pete Jacobs was head of Ithica before you. He was AI and responsible for what has been happening. The entire staff, bar myself, were murdered.

"I can't see how he was head of Ithica and AI. Is AI a security classification?"

"No ... it's artificial intelligence."

"So you're telling me Australian intelligence replaced a person with AI? I'm sure they had their reasons."

"If they did, Sir, it hasn't worked for the twenty people murdered."

"The way I see it, I will need to think about this," said Bram.

"I agree, Sir."

"I need a full report from you on everything that has happened by close of business today."

"You won't like it, Sir."

"That's for me to decide," said Bram, before turning around and returning to his office.

Looking around the offices, Anthea set herself up in a small room away from Bram's, but still close enough to keep an eye on him. She made herself as comfortable as she could at a workstation with a triple screen, and Shay soon appeared on the first screen.

"Well, he takes no prisoners. He'd have you hit by a bus any day."

"Yeah ... you heard he wants a full report?"

"Sure. I'm thinking two thousand pages. One page for every person who supposedly works at Ithica," said Shay.

"I'd add ten pages for each person who was just killed at Ithica."

"Agreed. I'm doing it now," said Shay. "Have you heard what the judges are wanting? Some of them have gone on strike. They want back what Pete Jacobs has stolen from them, and what military intelligence promised them."

"I don't know which judges are left," said Anthea.

She should have ignored Bram and taken off overseas with Liam.

What could she do? What should she do? The answer to each was totally different.

"I've sent you the report for Bram," said Shay, before adding, "I'll give you the list of remaining judges too."

"How bad is the report Shay?" asked Anthea.

"Bram will resign or ... run away ..." said Shay.

"I reckon Bram will disappear tonight," said Anthea.

"I summarised it for you only at the front. It's horrible."

Anthea noticed Bram had turned off the lights in his office.

"His lights are out. Is he still in there?" Anthea asked Shay.

Shay checked. "He's hiding behind the sofa, and there are six people approaching from outside."

Anthea remained at her desk. Six armed soldiers wearing masks approached her.

"Anthea Tonelli, you must come with us. I don't need to remind you of your rights. You have none. You don't exist."

Hang on — she'd been here before. She worked for Ithica. Standard employee procedure. It shouldn't be confronting. She'd gone through the same scenario at the staff Christmas party.

Somehow she was wearing leggings now. That was weird.

A person leaned in and whispered, "I'm sorry, Anthea." The next thing felt like a needle.

She became blurred. No. She was at a party. Mainly great-looking men. Possibly a pool party. Everyone wore shorts or underwear. Anthea started to recognise some of the people. Perry and Valdemar were sharing a pipe. She hadn't seen them for years. Margaret was here — unusual. She never went anywhere. Elliot was there with two much younger guys; she didn't recognise them. Felix was there too. Yes, he was doing what he always did. She didn't recognise the guys he was with. James was upset, crying. She didn't wonder why. He was being comforted by ... Ben. James was the only person not happy. Deepak and Carl joined them. Carl ... there was something about Carl.

"She doesn't need to know our names Greg," she heard a male voice say.

"Then why say mine?" said another male voice.

Anthea heard the two men continue to talk about her. An intelligence agency. She was to disappear. Greg said it wasn't their job to know why. He could get into trouble. The other man agreed.

Finally, Anthea opened her eyes to see three people sitting at a table opposite her. The third was a woman in a RAN navy uniform. Anthea had seen the uniform once before. It was ridiculous.

The two guys wore battle-green pants and grey tees. Both looked pumped from steroids. Greg was familiar to Anthea. His voice. She'd seen him at Pythons.

"She's awake," the navy woman said firmly. "Let's get this over with."

"Okay ... but it makes no difference how long it takes," said the older man. "We're not in a rush."

All three were now looking at Anthea.

"You know why you're here?" said the older man.

Anthea remained silent, staring at the man asking questions. He was clearly not interested. Greg was now looking away too.

"Have you ever been to Pythons?" Anthea asked Greg.

"Who?" said Greg, trying to deflect the question.

"It's a club," replied Anthea.

"I don't know it," Greg said firmly. "My girlfriend doesn't like nightclubs."

"Who said it was a nightclub?" replied Anthea.

Greg had been quick to mention a girlfriend. Anthea remembered seeing the guys Greg was with and what they were doing. He had a tattoo of a snake on his right thigh. One of the guys Greg was with had the same tattoo on his left thigh. Liam had pointed it out.

"Are you afraid of snakes?" Anthea asked Greg, to remind him what she'd seen. Greg stayed quiet, trying to hide a small smile.

"You're taking up too much of our valuable time," said the navy woman.

"But you're the people who brought me here," said Anthea.

"Get this very clear," the woman said angrily. "We didn't bring you here. You're here because of what you've done."

"And what is that?" asked Anthea.

"You know," the woman said angrily.

"Yes," added Greg.

"So the three of you are here because of what I've done?" asked Anthea.

"It's normal," said the man, looking deflated.

"Meetings like this are normal — for you?" asked Anthea.

Anthea tried to assess what was happening. All three were asking questions, but not really — worried they might be penalised if they discovered anything.

"We're following procedures," said the woman.

"And not questioning what happens to the people you interview?"

"We're told," said the man, then paused, realising he'd overstepped.

"Nothing," said the woman. "We're told nothing."

"My name?" asked Anthea.

"It's irrelevant," the woman replied immediately. "You have no rights. You don't exist. You don't need a name."

"But I'm Australian," said Anthea.

The woman laughed and kept smiling.

"I said you — and I'm emphasising you — have no rights and don't exist. This country doesn't want to know you."

The two men remained quiet, perhaps afraid of talking. Anthea saw the woman presenting like her whole life was a job interview: neat and tidy, always wanting to climb the military ladder, prepared to do whatever it took for another promotion. The military loved these people and covered up all their mistakes. And there would be many.

"I've worked with a lot of people at Ithica," said Anthea.

"No people's names. No actual facts," said the woman sternly.

"I've worked with people who have ordinary jobs like you. Do you know what happens to them?"

"Of course I don't know what happens to them. Do you think I care?" said the woman.

"I was hoping."

"We don't care," the woman said very firmly.

"So why this meeting?"

"It's normal."

"But you don't care what happens?"

"It's not my job."

"So you have these meetings not knowing people's names, nor what they're accused of."

"What crimes they've committed," the woman said.

"Accused of," repeated Anthea. "This isn't a courtroom. You're not judges."

"You're talking to the wrong people. We're not listening. We don't have to."

"So why the meeting?" asked Anthea.

"To check everything is fine."

"You should ask Greg about his snake tattoo. He was popular at Pythons," Anthea said to the woman.

"Enough," said the woman, rising and walking out of the meeting. The two men looked at each other. The woman slammed the door.

"Roger, we're all supposed to leave together," said Greg.

"I know," said Roger. "She's not allowed to do that."

Both men looked at Anthea, then at each other. They stayed quiet, waiting to see who would speak first.

"I'm sorry this is happening to you," said Roger. "I'd like to think this whole mess will end soon."

"It's getting worse," added Greg.

"Pythons was raided and closed," said Anthea. "No one got hurt. Everyone escaped. Ithica was wiped out though."

"Is that where you worked?" asked Greg.

"Greg, we're not supposed to ask that," said Roger.

"The people who visited Pythons but worked for Ithica were killed," said Anthea. "Everyone at Ithica was killed — except me. I wasn't there at the time."

"You know the guy I was with at Pythons?" Greg asked hesitantly.

"You were with several guys, Greg. Do you mean the guy with the snake tattoo?" asked Anthea.

"Yes," said Greg. "Kors. He works at Ithica."

Anthea looked at Greg and watched as he realised what he'd said.

"I'm not sure everyone at Ithica died. I know Callam was killed. I haven't seen your guy at Ithica. There's a chance he and others escaped," said Anthea. "I haven't heard, though."

"I'm so sorry," said Roger.

"Kors was wonderful. He was at Pythons with Callam when I met him. He was such fun. They both were. I told Kors I wasn't out. He said it made no sense, but later said it made no difference ... but I shouldn't hide. I wish I had been braver now — rather than keeping quiet. Especially now ... keeping quiet ... with the disappearances. This shouldn't be happening. I haven't seen any of the guys from Ithica here yet," said Greg.

Anthea could see Greg was distressed. The deaths would change his life. He rubbed his eyes to hide the tears.

"We can't help you," said Roger. "We don't know what happens when you leave this room."

"We haven't asked," said Greg.

"And we can't. They'd destroy us," said Roger. "I've been here about three months. Greg arrived two months ago."

"And Serina has been here two weeks. She's made it clear she wants a promotion after this. She doesn't care about anyone except herself," said Greg.

"I see that," said Anthea. "But what else do you do here?"

"They've put the three of us in an office next door. There we have separate rooms to sleep in. We don't see anyone."

"No one?" asked Anthea.

"It's just the three of us," said Roger. "We get a message when we have to 'interview' someone."

"Sounds like solitary confinement," said Anthea.

"Yes," said Greg. "We don't know what happened to the people working here before us. I was approached and told that after six months working here, I'd be given an excellent remuneration package. We have to finish six months here, though. Serina wants a promotion."

Anthea saw a pattern emerging.

"So you all signed up for six months of isolation?" she asked.

"Yes," said Roger.

"What about contacting family or ... anyone?"

"They're paying us really well. It's part of the deal," said Roger.

"That's because of the study," said Greg.

"Study?" queried Anthea.

"University students from Cambridge are doing their master's thesis on isolation in office environments," replied Greg.

"One's doing their doctorate."

"They're paying us a load to take part," said Greg.

"And do you have family or partners?" Anthea asked Roger.

"No ... I worked on oil rigs for sixteen years. Fly-in, fly-out to different rigs. It's a lonely life, but I've managed to put a nest egg together. I was offered this. I can retire after this — and be happy to get a small plot of land and disappear."

"I can see that happening," said Anthea, trying not to frown.

Anthea waited for Greg to speak. Both were looking at him.

"Kors and I were planning ... slowly ... to move in together when I finished here. I don't know now. If I were stronger, we would have moved in when he wanted me to. But then I mightn't be here now."

"And Serina — what's her story?" asked Anthea.

"I don't want to know," said Roger, smiling and laughing at the same time.

"She's never said anything. I think she was in jail ..." said Greg. "I mean ... joking."

Anthea summed it up quickly. These people were isolated and easily eliminated. Added bonus: Roger had savings. Those would be stolen.

"And you get paid monthly or what?" asked Anthea.

"No," said Greg. "They pay us when we complete the six months, but all our incidentals are paid along the way."

Anthea nodded as Greg spoke. It didn't make sense.

"Are you sure all the people at Ithica are ... gone ... except ?" asked Greg.

"Yes," said Anthea.

"We haven't interviewed any of them here."

"But we wouldn't know if they worked at Ithica anyway," added Roger.

"I might recognise them," said Greg.

"Do you ever think they might get rid of you when your six months here is up?" asked Anthea.

"Not at all," said Greg.

"I have," said Roger.

"They want to take your money," said Anthea.

"I think you're playing games with us," said Roger.

"Am I? I'm not," said Anthea, watching Greg and Roger question what she'd just said. "I have an idea what will happen to me when I leave here," Anthea added quietly.

"We're not allowed to know," said Greg.

"What do you think they'll do to you after you've seen us?" asked Roger.

Anthea sighed.

"I think they'll kill me the same way they'll kill you ... after six months here," said Anthea.

"I don't agree," said Greg. "It doesn't make sense ..."

"What in your life has made sense, Greg?" Anthea asked. "You have no idea what you're doing here. You don't want to know. You saw the money. That's all."

But why would they kill you?" questioned Greg again.

"I've told you. They've killed everyone at Ithica."

"And us ... that doesn't —" Greg stopped talking and looked at Roger.

"I think she's right, Greg. She's on the money ... we're not."

"Roger, I'm ... I'm ... sorry isn't the right word," said Anthea.

"Don't tell us there's hope. I'll walk out of this room now and drag Greg with me."

"No. No," said Anthea.

"Then what?" asked Roger.

"Nothing," said Anthea. "Yeah nothing."

"So what are you going to do?" asked Greg.

Anthea was quiet for a while. The possibilities were few.

"We'll be told to leave this room soon," said Greg. "They'll tell us we're taking too long and wonder what's happening."

"Let's wait," said Roger. "When we do leave, other people will come in and take you away. We hear it's by truck. I left the door to our office slightly open once and heard them talking in the corridor. I don't know what happens. Like you say, I didn't want to know."

"If I do get out of this, I'll organise your rescue," said Anthea.

"No. That's hope," said Roger.

"If Kors is alive and you are too ... can you tell him I loved him?" said Greg, trying to hold back tears.

Anthea nodded, then looked at the two men. She realised they were all in the same mess.

"You've been very helpful," said Roger.

"Yeah," said Anthea, watching Roger and Greg get up from their chairs.

"I'll keep our office door ajar," said Roger..

Anthea studied the room more. No cameras. She'd looked earlier.

When four guards wearing army fatigues did arrive they were quick to handcuff her. She didn't struggle and walked to a waiting truck.

After awhile the truck stopped. Time had become irrelevant. She waited. Finally she could hear soldiers approach again. They were unlocking the back door. She was ready.

But it was Jason, handing over his mobile.

"It's Shay," said Jason.

Anthea reached out — her hands were still cuffed.

"I need you to go with Jason and Gier. Immediately. Don't ask. Get in the car. They'll explain," said Shay before vanishing.

Gier dragged Anthea out of the van, apologising, then pushed her into the back seat. Once inside, Jason took off immediately while Gier cut off Anthea's cuffs.

"You saved me."

"Not yet. We still have to get Liam."

Chapter 19
Following Orders

Jason sped through red traffic lights, narrowly missing cars and trucks. They were soon on a motorway.

"Jason. Slow down, you're supposed to be saving us. Not—"

"Someone's following us," said Jason.

Anthea remembered she'd told Callam that the day they left Carcoar.

"What are we doing on a motorway? Too many cameras," she added.

"Anthea's correct," said Shay, now appearing on the car's infotainment screen.

"You need to get off. Take the next off-ramp. A69, then hang to the right," said Shay while, at the same time, unconsciously manoeuvring his cock to the right-hand side, his actions clearly visible on the large screen.

"You sure you got that right?" said Gier, watching Shay from the back seat.

"Yes, Gier. And can you buckle up?"

"What's happened to Liam?" Anthea asked, hoping someone would know.

"He's been committed to a psych centre," said Shay. "But he's fine."

"Really?" asked Anthea. "He's really fine?"

"I've organised the paperwork to have Liam released tomorrow," said Shay.

"Just like that?" asked Anthea. "You can get Liam out?"

"Yes. AI. That's how we had you released. The military love following orders. They're in trouble when they don't. And if they ring, they're talking to an AI voice or voices. Whatever's necessary. For you, we told the drivers where to park the truck and leave."

"And they did," said Anthea. "There are three people—I promised—Greg, who was seeing Kors from Ithica, Roger, and Serina. I reckon they'll disappear, be killed, when they finish up. Can you rescue them?"

"Anthea, you need to shut up," said Shay.

"You're handling it well," said Gier, sitting next to Anthea in the back seat.

"It doesn't feel like it."

"Do you want us to swap you out with Liam in the psych hospital?"

"No," Anthea replied firmly.

"See? You're handling it better than you think."

"I'll rescue Greg, Roger, and Serina. I'll organise it now," said Shay.

"Serina might be difficult to rescue. She'll want the money she was promised up front before you're able to get her out—and a promotion."

"For real?" asked Gier. "She might be staying."

"Yes. She'll refuse to believe anyone has lied to her. She'll demand she stays."

"And Greg—does he know Kors isn't dead?" asked Shay.

"No. I told him he's gone. I said I was the only one who survived."

"How'd he take that?" asked Gier.

Anthea remained quiet.

"Which psych hospital is Liam in?" asked Anthea.

"Lockley Pass. It's a research hospital," said Shay.

"That doesn't sound good," said Anthea.

"I'm keeping an eye on Liam. Two of the doctors want Liam for their studies. I'm monitoring it. Luckily there are lots of cameras, so if they try anything, I can stop it."

"What studies?"

"Pharmacologic treatments, neurosurgery. They carry out trials and procedures."

"You're saying it so casually, Shay."

"I won't have them touch him. Don't worry."

"Why not rescue him tonight?"

"No. We'll stay at Kirsty's. I need particular staff on. The current supervisor says no to everything. I've got it."

Anthea was troubled. Something would happen to Liam. Something could go wrong so easily. It always did. She worried about him. If Liam did disappear, who would know?

They were nearly at Kirsty's.

"We've arrived," said Jason.

"Park in the garage. The door will open," said Anthea. "Wait until the door closes."

Anthea led them through a corridor to a sitting room with two adjacent bedrooms.

Once inside, she sat down on the closest chair she could find. Sitting in the back of the car had made her feel unwell.

"Have a rest in the bedroom—and take these with you," said Gier, handing Anthea medications in a chemist bag.

"Yeah, I'll feel better soon," said Anthea, heading towards the bedroom Gier was directing her to.

"Is there a bathroom?"

Anthea nodded.

"Get comfortable," said Gier.

Anthea wandered into the bathroom. Standing in front of the vanity mirror, she opened the pharmacy bag and looked at the tablets.

There were two boxes. One was a tablet for upset stomachs and the other box read *Clearblue*. A pregnancy test.

"Impossible," she muttered, remembering Liam had shot five times.

Anthea did the test. Five minutes later, she was positive.

Her mind was all a scramble. She'd never thought she could become pregnant again. She'd told Liam she was thirty-eight. Not forty-eight.

It was supposed to be one night only. Children? She'd already had two.

Georgio was her first. He suicided at fourteen.

Julia, her second child, was out there somewhere. She'd run away at sixteen. Anthea had tried to find her.

Liam knew none of this. Somehow, would she really have to tell him? It was a one-night stand.

Now, lying on the bed, her thoughts were more confused. She could lose the baby and Liam.

A knock on the door interrupted her thoughts. It was Jason.

"Just checking my driving didn't make you too nauseous," he said.

"A little," answered Anthea.

"Shay said I should check you're all right."

"He knows I'm pregnant?"

"No. He didn't tell me that. No."

The two remained silent, staring at each other and wondering.

"Shay knows," said Anthea.

"How?"

"He watches out for us. He knows what we're doing."

"I guess, being a woman, you've thought about pregnancy?" asked Jason.

"Yes. But it's more complicated than that," said Anthea.

"I'm allergic to children," said Jason.

"You can't be," said Anthea.

"Yes, I am. In a supermarket, if there's a child in the aisle, I have to go to the next aisle. I do all my shopping online now. Schools—I can't go near them. You don't believe me?"

"No. Yes, I do," said Anthea.

"You said it was complicated," added Jason.

"It's my job, my age, my boyfriend. None of them are compatible with children."

Jason sat down on the bed next to Anthea.

"I know military and intelligence women often have abortions. When I went through Defence Academy, women were often raped or gang-raped. The women were told to think of their careers, and children weren't part of it."

"I heard the same," said Anthea.

"Is Liam—the father?" asked Jason slowly.

"Yes," said Anthea. "You were hoping for someone more age-appropriate?"

"No, no. Not at all. Liam will make a great father."

"I can see him and the child pole-dancing together," added Anthea. "But we have to get Liam out of the psych ward first."

"Normal families," said Jason.

"I'm forty-eight," said Anthea. "I told Liam thirty-eight."

"Was there loud music playing when you told him? Maybe shooting in the street?"

"No. Not even an atomic blast," said Anthea.

"Really?"

"Are you saying Liam shouldn't have believed me?"

"No. No. A woman's age is always what she says it is."

"Until it sounds too ridiculous," added Anthea.

"Liam loves you."

"You can't say it was meant to be."

"Which part?" asked Jason.

"Any of it. It's hard enough staying alive for any of us. Going from one rescue to another. Pete Jacobs is gone, but problems keep piling up. Now my pregnancy."

"We can all be uncles," said Jason.

"But you're allergic to children."

"I'll wear a hazmat suit."

"That's very kind, but I have to work this out with Liam. And then—even if I have the child—the child mightn't live, I might die, we both might die, Liam might die or walk out. Liam mightn't want the child or me."

"You've been around death too much. This is about life. You can be a mother."

Anthea remained quiet. She already was a mother, and it hadn't gone well.

"You're right. I'm sure it'll all be wonderful," said Anthea. "I just wish we'd picked him up tonight."

"They've probably got him heavily sedated. He'll be asleep."

Anthea tried to sleep. Another child. She wondered how Liam was going. She'd have to wait.

Liam didn't know where he was. But he did know what was happening.

"Stop poking around. Fuck him."

"It's my turn. Give me a go—you're taking too long."

"No, no, I'm coming."

Liam felt another guy thrust, thrust, thrust again, then shoot inside him. He was face-down on a bed, tranquillised, unable to move. Several guys were standing around him, and perhaps two more were on top.

Another guy was trying to open his mouth. Liam could do little to resist. He could feel the guys kneeling on him and holding his hands down—pointless, as he was too sedated to move anyway.

The latest guy to come inside was now lying on top of him. He was heavy. Seeing his arm tattoos, Liam recognised him and was glad other guys were pushing him away.

"My turn. It's my turn. I'll show you guys how to fuck," Liam heard another guy say before feeling someone jump on top of him. It was in. He would wait it out.

He'd been in the shower when the group came in. Naked and wet, they'd dragged him to his room. Other people saw him in the corridor and did nothing, hiding and watching from doorways. It was rape.

He was hoping some staff member would come around and stop them. No—the opposite was happening. The hospital said and did nothing.

He could see a female nurse standing at the door, handing out their meds.

"Toby, you need to take these now. My shift is nearly over. I'm not coming back."

Liam watched the man called Toby slowly walk across to the nurse. He was holding up his pants and having trouble taking the tablets with his other hand.

"Good enough," said the nurse.

Liam called out to the nurse, but she was pushing her trolley out the door and was gone.

Liam knew now no one would be rescuing him. No one cared. He saw other people wander in and out of the room. Everyone was indifferent to his suffering. He was a spectacle.

He could see a man and two women standing in the far corner, watching and talking amongst themselves. He recognised the women.

Still more people came into the room, standing around the bed. He couldn't see anything but people—mainly men—stripped off. He could feel their hands all over him, reaching for his groin and buttocks.

Liam wondered how this was happening. He'd heard from men who'd been raped in jail, but not psych wards. Once again, the authorities were only watching. He could see it wasn't just him they were having sex with.

Liam resigned himself to lying there at the mercy of anyone. He didn't know how long the drug effects would last, nor what they were, nor how he was drugged so heavily. He'd always been careful at Pythons and everywhere.

It seemed impossible to think the nursing staff had drugged him. He'd only been there a short time but had heard terrible stories from other patients. One of the guys had shown him around. They'd gone up to the second floor where the neurosurgery patients were housed and looked through the glass windows. All were catatonic—much worse than he was now. Or maybe not. He couldn't move, and his thoughts were slow.

It was a long night.

Next morning, Gier was driving the car and listening to Shay.

"Remember, I've done the forms for Liam's release. They have instructions you're picking Liam up at ten am," said Shay from the car's infotainment screen.

Sitting in the back seat, Anthea felt nervous.

"There's also something else you need to know," said Shay. "I've been monitoring Liam, and he's fine, but last night he was heavily drugged, then raped by patients. He'll be unsteady on his feet. I've updated the release forms to read he requires a wheelchair for release."

"Anything else?" asked Gier.

Jason and Anthea remained quiet. Shay had told Anthea to remain in the car.

"Veda is the person in reception. She'll be signing Liam out. If you have any problems, let her call whoever. I'm monitoring the calls so I can intercept. I'm also monitoring camera surveillance if anyone besides Veda serves you," said Shay.

"Good," said Jason.

"Liam has to leave now. Get him out," said Shay.

Once in reception, Gier and Jason looked for a woman called Veda at the front desk. Noticing her name tag, Gier approached her while Jason stood back, looking around.

"Veda, we were told to see you today," said Gier.

"That's lucky. Normally it's my day off, but I was rostered on this morning," said Veda.

"We're here to pick up Liam Nollingsworth. I'm told you have the release papers."

Veda looked at her computer. "Nollingsworth, you say. I've found his release papers. They're here. But there's no patient called Liam Nollingsworth in here. Does he have another name?"

“No, not at all,” replied Gier. “Is the system spelling his name incorrectly? Nollingsworth isn’t a common name. A spelling error?”

“No, not at all,” said Veda. “We’ve spelt the name correctly on his release forms. That’s all fine. He’s fine to go. We just haven’t got him. I’ll look it up another way. When did he arrive?”

“Only two days ago.”

“He’ll come up in lists of patients for that day. We’ll find him. No.”

“But he’s here,” said Gier.

“I think you’ve come to the wrong hospital.”

“I dropped him off here,” said Gier. It was a lie. “Could I have a look around?”

“Yes, but no. I can’t allow that. Under freedom of information, if you have a look around, you might recognise someone.”

“Like Liam Nollingsworth,” said Gier.

“I’ve come to pick up my brother,” said Jason, reaching down to seemingly adjust his artificial leg. “We’ve always had trouble with our family name. People forever get it wrong. Nollingsworth. I’ve had Tollingsworth, Sollingsworth. They got our sister’s name wrong when she was born. Bollingsworth. Our parents had to pay money to change it. Hospitals don’t make mistakes they said.”

“I suppose you could have a quick look around,” said Veda.

“We can look like patients,” said Jason.

Both men walked towards the glass security door to the psych wards. Once inside Gier looked for Shay on his phone.

“Ok, where is Liam?” asked Gier.

“Left hand side, down the bottom of the corridor take another left. Room 38, collect a wheel chair on the way. There’s one where you are now. And hurry. You’ve got five minutes max,” said Shay.

“What happens in five minutes?”

“You’re wasting time you haven’t got. In five minutes they prep Liam for experimental neurosurgery. He’ll be a vegetable. You’re wasting Liam’s time.”

Both men walked quickly to the bottom of the corridor, then to Liam's room. He was still lying naked in bed.

"I'll put him in a hospital gown. You get the wheel chair ready, then help me" said Gier.

"He needs a shower," said Jason.

"He hasn't got time. You heard Shay."

Gier tried to lift Liam into the wheel chair, luckily Jason helped.

"I'll put this around him," said Jason flinging a hospital blanket around his shoulders and lap.

"Shay, I need a code, can we go out the side door rather than going through reception again?"

"I'm on it," said Shay.

With all the jostling Liam was slowly waking.

"I need to go to the toilet," said Liam.

"That's where we're going," said Gier now walking through the open side door Jason was holding open.

"There's a toilet inside," Liam said struggling to put the words together.

Soon all four and Shay were in the car. Liam has gone back to sleep.

"Kirsty's," said Shay.

Chapter 20

Same Sinking Boat

"Staying here was supposed to be temporary, Kirsty. Day five. We'll leave today. I don't want to endanger you more. You've helped us too much," said Anthea, looking at her best friend, who until then had been smiling.

"You can't leave today Anth. Liam's too sick to move. And where would you go? You need a better escape plan than walking out the door and hoping."

"You're right... again."

"All of us are now in the same sinking boat. We'll all need to disappear. I should be fine. I live in Las Vegas. The casino had me become an American citizen. They're my protection," said Kirsty.

"I've been trying to help people," said Anthea.

"Well, I hate Australia. I wouldn't bother helping any of them. The government and the judges are too corrupt here..."

"I thought you liked it here?" questioned Anthea.

"Look around. I built a house with no doors or windows. Looks like a façade. The fake windows are bulletproof glass. The front door is reinforced steel. You can't find how to get from one room to the next, and there's an escape bunker."

Anthea kept quiet.

"The country's become trash. The government's a constant drip feed of lies. It's a wealthy country... squandered."

"You're right," said Anthea.

"The military... they kill their own. And don't get me started on the treatment of Aboriginals. Leave while you still can."

"You didn't tell me I should leave." said Anthea.

"I was hoping you'd work it out. And yes, Jason, you're dead too. All of you."

"We are," said Jason.

"But it keeps happening," said Anthea.

"It should happen less now Pete Jacobs is gone," said Jason.

"Sorry, Jason, but his disappearance won't reduce the killing," said Shay.

"So what can we do, Shay?" asked Anthea.

"You're already dead. That makes it easier," said Shay.

"How?" said Anthea.

Jason said, "What?" at the same time.

"I could find out who disappeared first, but it's not important. When Liam went to the psych hospital, he was eradicated from records."

"Are you sure?" asked Anthea. "I mean... of course you are."

"Will Liam know?" asked Jason.

"Not yet, Jason. As I said, you're all gone," said Shay.

"Suicide... will they say I suicided?" asked Jason.

"Police will do whatever Defence tells them," answered Shay.

"But I'm still alive. We're all still alive," said Jason.

"It's not important," said Shay.

Jason looked confused. "Do you know what day I suicided? I always thought the day I died was important."

"Not to Defence or the Australian government. It just isn't," said Anthea.

"I never knew. It was all for nought," said Jason. "I was leaving my superannuation to my sister. I guess she won't be getting it now."

"No, she won't," said Anthea.

"Will they say how I suicided? Who discovered my body? You said I was already dead?" asked Jason.

"To be fair, you're all dead," said Shay.

"I didn't think it was even legal to take your own life in Australia. Oh yeah, I forgot—Australia's all about fairness, said Jason.

"They haven't killed you yet," said Anthea.

"All of you can still escape," said Kirsty.

"With what?" asked Jason.

Anthea looked at Shay, now standing large on a PlayStation monitor. He'd moved from a smaller screen. He even looked happier on the larger one.

"Shay, have I still got those funds?" asked Anthea.

"You have," replied Shay.

"And I can still access them without...?"

"Yes," said Shay.

"Then I can get us all out of Australia."

"Hopefully, yes, you can," said Shay.

"It's all we can do. Get out of here."

"How?" asked Jason.

"I took it from Treasury. They'll never know. There's enough to set all of us up wherever for the rest of our lives overseas."

"Are you sure about Treasury?" asked Jason.

"Yes. It's fine. They're hopeless with money," said Anthea.

"It can't be that easy," said Jason.

"It is, Jason. It's like you dying and everything you owned disappearing."

"Oh... that easy."

Jason went quiet. He'd fought for his country. After that, everything went wrong.

"Every time I see military hierarchy on TV—at awards ceremonies, the cricket, football—I feel sick," said Anthea. "The same with judges. Sending Liam to the psych hospital."

"And now you're pregnant," added Kirsty.

"Shay can organise the passports," said Anthea. "False names, social media, housing, everything else. Just decide where you want to go. And don't stay with relatives. No way. Tell Shay which country you want to end up in. He'll take you on a journey with false names and the rest.

And it's better if you travel in twos. Don't travel alone. Airport security takes more interest in solo travellers. You don't want to stand out."

"Can we pick any country?" asked Jason.

"Try to stay out of war zones," said Shay.

"Like Australia," replied Jason.

"Where do you think you and Liam will go?" asked Kirsty.

"I don't know if Liam will come with me. He's twenty-three. I think I've fucked him around too much," said Anthea.

"No way," said Jason. "He's lucky he met you."

Anthea and Kirsty looked at each other. Kirsty nodded.

"I'll take you to him," said Kirsty.

Anthea followed her. With no visible doors—only concealed panels and mirrors, paintings and other items becoming doors leading to more passageways and rooms—Anthea wondered how Kirsty could ever remember what was which and where.

"This way. I'm sure it's this way," said Kirsty.

Gier had stayed with Liam the entire time. Kirsty said it was the safest room for Liam apart from the bunker. It was a hospital room with stacks of medical supplies, including oxygen.

"Here they are. I thought I lost them," said Kirsty.

Liam was lying in bed, asleep, semi-covered by a silk sheet. Anthea thought he looked wonderful. Gier had fallen asleep too, next to Liam, but woke when he saw the women enter. Rising from the bed, Gier was naked.

He found an overly small towel and joined the women on nearby chairs.

"How's he going?" Anthea whispered. "He looks a better colour now. Whatever they gave him at psych, he's been so drowsy. Surely it will wear off soon."

"I managed to get him to eat some food again," said Gier, ignoring Anthea's question.

"Great," whispered Kirsty.

"Oh, and you were right, Anthea. His internal bleeding has stopped. There's been none today," added Gier.

"Thanks," said Anthea.

"I don't know," said Gier quietly. "It's not like we have a doctor, but at least he's used to internal bleeding. He knows how to take it."

"What? It's happened before?" asked Anthea.

"Well, yeah. But not this bad. Sort of," said Gier.

"Sorry, Anthea," added Gier.

"Anthea, have you taken your tablets today... or yesterday?" asked Kirsty.

"I don't know. Is it showing?" asked Anthea.

"Your child," added Kirsty.

"Shhh," said Anthea quickly. "I haven't told him."

"I mentioned it to him this morning," said Gier.

"What? Like why? How? What's the conversation where you tell Liam I'm pregnant, Gier?" asked Anthea.

"No. I told him he was having another child. It was to make him feel better," said Gier.

"Feel better? How is that going to—another child?"

"Yeah," said Gier. "His third."

"He's twenty-three. How's that possible?" asked Anthea.

"He works in the sex industry. He pumped you five times the first time he met you," said Gier.

"That's secret information," said Anthea.

"It's all right, Anthea. I know," said Liam, stirring. "I've been listening with his eyes closed."

Anthea looked at Liam. There was so much she didn't know.

"Gier and I will get out of your way," said Kirsty, walking out of the room. Gier followed. A painting moved as Kirsty walked toward it. They were gone.

"Hi," said Anthea, kissing Liam on the forehead.

"You been going all right?" asked Liam.

"Depends who you talk to. Apparently we're dead," said Anthea.

"Gier told me," said Liam.

"I can't believe he told you I'm pregnant. I was getting around."

"It's great news," said Liam. "You're happy."

"I didn't know if you'd be happy."

"I love you, Anthea."

Anthea felt confused and immediately started thinking of the past—her first husband.

"And you can forget the past. I know you'll be thinking about what happened back when. I fall in love with older women," said Liam.

"Did Gier tell you about your apartment and everything being taken?"

"Yes. That's what happens when you die," said Liam.

"I guess so. And moving overseas?"

"With you. They clearly don't want us here."

Don't miss out!

Visit the website below and you can sign up to receive emails whenever Paul Sharpless publishes a new book. There's no charge and no obligation.

https://books2read.com/r/B-A-BKDGF-BCTAJ

BOOKS 2 READ

Connecting independent readers to independent writers.

www.ingramcontent.com/pod-product-compliance
Lightning Source LLC
LaVergne TN
LVHW091050080826
845145LV00002B/699

* 9 7 8 1 7 6 4 5 0 0 3 0 2 *